To Adam

o l

The Young American Series
Book 1

Runs With The Wind

By
John L. Hough

Renegade Publishing
P.O. Box 544
Camp Verde, AZ 86322

www.RenegadePublishing.com

Cover Art by: Betty Ramirez-Atkins
32281 Hwy 160
Cortez, CO 81321
FAX 970-565-2339

NON STRIPABLE COVER

THE YOUNG AMERICAN SERIES
BOOK 1
RUNS WITH THE WIND
PUBLISHED BY

Renegade Publishing
P.O. Box 544
Camp Verde, AZ 86322

www.RenegadePublishing.com

Copyright 2000 by John L. Hough
Printed in the United States of America
Library of Congress Card Number: 00-191940
ISBN-0-97404050-1-4

Chapter One

Who would have thought, on that cold and dreary April morning in St. Louis when I poked my head out from under the quilt Ma had made for me, that my wildest dreams of adventure were about to become a reality. The sky was becoming light enough to see that the low moving dark grey clouds had not yet given way to the sun. It was warm and cozy under the handstitched quilt, and I hated to leave it for the misting rain that had plagued us for the last several days, but I knew it was time to get busy. This was the day I had been waiting for. Yawning and stretching I lay there thinking about how this had all come to pass.

Almost a month earlier our destiny was decided by fate, and there was nothing we could have done to stop it. The only home I had ever known stood on a small bench on the west side of what had always been a peaceful little creek. It was a nice place to live, with sprawling shade trees on each side of the house. On the front was a large porch facing east where Ma and Pa sat drinking coffee as they watched the sunrise each morning. On the east side of the creek the land rose slightly to a small grove of walnut trees where it then dropped off in the typical fashion of the rolling landscape. The barn and corrals were set closer to the creek in the bottom land, with a chicken coup built against the west side. Life was simple then, at least until it started to rain day after day.

The night the flood came, I woke up to hear Pa burst through the door of the house yelling, "Cheryl, wake up the kids and have Jeremy hitch the wagon. It's a flood, the biggest I've ever seen."

In minutes we were dressed, and while Misty and Ma gathered the necessities and valuables I ran out to hitch the wagon, working faster than I had ever worked before. I was fourteen at the time and nearly as big as Pa, so the hard work didn't bother me, it was the urgency in his voice that scared me, I had never known him to be afraid of anything. Pa was doing his best to find the livestock, but he wasn't having much luck in the driving rain.

As I led the team and wagon out of the barn, lightning lit up the sky sending eerie shadows dancing through the night. In the flash I could see the few cows we owned standing in the grove of walnut trees on the far side of what used to be the peaceful little creek. The ground where they stood wasn't much more than five feet above the normal water line and they were already belly deep in fast moving water. You couldn't even tell they were standing on that little swell. Pa hollered for me to put the rest of the horses on lead ropes while they loaded the wagon, so I headed back through the darkness to the barn.

It all seemed like a bad dream. We had endured floods before, but nothing like this one. The thunder boomed so loud it seemed to echo in my head, and the raging wind was ripping limbs out of the massive cottonwood trees all around us.

I brought out Pa's saddle horse, Star, a big black stallion with a white blaze on his forehead. I had barely gotten him tied to the wagon before a bolt of lightning ripped through the night shattering a huge oak tree near the barn. He reared back and jerked his head violently letting out a frightened scream. With eyes as big as goose eggs, and nostrils flared, he looked like he had seen the devil himself, but the knot held fast, and I went after the other horse, Renegade. This was the horse Pa had broke for me the summer before, and we had become the best of friends. I tied him next to Star, and it was easy to see, the stallion sired good stock. Renegade was a chestnut gelding, the color of his mother but with Star's white blaze and size. Both horses were well muscled from many hours in the harness as well as the saddle.

With the wagon loaded we were ready to head for higher ground. We were trying to see how the cows were doing, but the rain was coming harder now and even in the lightning you couldn't see much, so we left everything I had ever known and headed for town.

It was three days before the water went down enough that we could get back to the farm. Pa and I rode out on the fourth morning to look around and I couldn't believe what I saw. There were huge cottonwood trees laying everywhere and a big pile of driftwood where the barn used to be. Several gullies had been cut in the fields, and the bottom lands were completely gutted. Even the apple trees, that Pa had planted there, were gone or uprooted, laying at odd angles, clinging desperately for life. Nothing but rocks and sand were left around their tangled roots.

We searched for two days but there was no sign of our cows, even most of the chickens were nowhere to be found.

The next morning I was sitting on the front steps of the bank enjoying the rare sunshine. Pa had gone inside to see about a loan to put the farm back in working order.

"John I'd like to give you the money," the banker said honestly, shuffling papers around his desk, "but I just can't."

Desperately, Pa looked across the desk at Mr. Peterson. "Why? You know I'm good for it. I've been working that farm for over twenty years."

"I know you are, but you've got to realize John, this flood hit just about everybody. There isn't enough money left to go around."

"That's just great," John said clutching his hat tightly in his powerful fist, "and what am I supposed to do now?"

"The best you can John, that's all any of us can do."

With that Pa came out of the bank. He stood there staring off in the distance saying nothing. I could tell that things had not gone well. After a few minutes he said, "Come on Jeremy, lets go to the livery and get the wagon."

"Are we going home Pa?"

"Yea, we got a lot of work to do," the words seemed heavy as he spoke them. It was as though he had lost all hope.

We headed down the street and turned the corner to the livery noticing a small crowd gathered in front. As we got closer I could hear someone talking with great enthusiasm.

He was a fascinating man with brown shoulder length hair, turning gray in places, and tied back with a leather thong. He wore dirty, beaded, buckskins with fringes down the arms and moccasins that came almost to his knees. His beard was mostly gray with a touch of brown tobacco stain right in the middle of it. He was loud and smelled a little, but he had a sort of confidence and charm that drew people in closer so they wouldn't miss a single word.

"It's all out there," he said, making a sweeping motion with his arm. "It's a big country fer men with dreams. Mountains so high they have snow on the tops all year long. Clear streams with water as sweet as honeysuckle. Beaver so thick you can't count 'em all, and buffalo, why there's so many that it sometimes takes two days just to ride around a single herd. There's land for the taking out there. Why it's Gods' country I tell ya."

"If it's so great, what are you doing in St. Louis?" one man asked.

"I got me a hankering to spend my poke on whiskey and fancy ladies, taint neither out there. Would be nice if there was though, I wouldn't have to come dragging myself clear cross the country every two or three years."

Pa and I stood there listening to him for quite a spell as he talked like a man who hadn't had any one to talk to for a long, long time. He told story after story capturing the imaginations of young and old alike.

"Stay here Jeremy," Pa said, "I'll be back in a bit. I've got some business to tend to." He left me standing there listening to the old mountain man telling stories about things I had never even dreamed of.

When he came back with Ma and Misty, I was standing in front of the livery with the wagon hitched and ready to go.

"Good. Let's go back to the farm and get the rest of our things," Pa said.

On the way back to the house he told me about how he had sold the farm to Mr. Peterson at the bank and made arrangements to buy a covered wagon from the freight company. Ma wasn't to happy about the idea at first, but after seeing what the flood had done to the farm, she knew why Pa just couldn't stay.

We gathered up the rest of our things and when a wagon train to the West started forming, Pa was one of the first to sign on. It had been four weeks now and the big day finally came, it was time to go, we were headed West. I jumped out of bed, dressing as fast as possible. I wanted to have the wagon hitched up and ready to go by the time Ma had breakfast ready.

Chapter Two

As we pulled up to the meeting place along the river, a group of men were gathering under a stand of cottonwood trees. It was plain to see they were in a pretty heated argument. Mr. Reeves, the wagon master was trying to calm them down but not having much luck. Being a small man, and sort of plain he lacked the self-confidence to overpower the crowd.

"Calm down," he yelled, "I've got this figured out."

But no one was listening to him. They just kept yelling louder and louder trying to be heard above the rest. Each man trying to make his point of view seem more important than the others.

That's when Jimmy stepped out of the trees behind the crowd. He was a tall, lean man, maybe two inches better than six feet and dressed like the mountain man Pa and I had seen at the livery a few weeks before. He had shoulder length blond hair and steel grey eyes. A square jaw and weathered face told of the hard life he had led. A reddish brown mustache, that drooped well below his chin, nearly concealed a ragged scar on his right cheek.

Jimmy drew out his pistol and fired a shot in the air, causing everybody's head to jerk around at once.

"That's enough," he said in an even tone, still holding his gun as if he meant business. As long as I'm the scout on this train, when Mr. Reeves talks, everybody listens. He's the man in charge. That's the way it was when you signed on, that's the way it'll be when you leave. If anyone wants to argue the point, now's the time, before we get started."

No one wanted to argue with Jimmy and Mr. Reeves was able to regain control of the meeting.

"Now then," he said, "it seems that everyone wants to be in the lead on this wagon train. Well, it can't be like that. So here's what we're going to do. There's twenty seven wagons signed up, so we'll put twenty seven numbers in the hat, and as I call your name, you'll draw the number and that will be your place in line."

As Mr. Reeves called the names, each man went up and drew his number and you could tell by the look on their faces whether it was high or low. Pa said it was just as well that we drew number ten, there wouldn't be as much dust as at the back of the train, and we wouldn't have to be the first to make the river crossings.

As the train started off Jimmy and Mr. Reeves took the lead. Jimmy was a man with a lot of self confidence, and when he started out, he never looked back. Mr. Reeves though, wasn't so sure of himself. He kept turning back and riding along the wagon train to make sure everything was going smoothly. One by one the wagons fell into place and began their journey across the rolling plains. The trail was well established here so the going was easy and we made pretty good time.

This gave us a chance to get to know the folks in front of us and those close behind. The two wagons right in front of us were one family so that actually put us as the eleventh wagon. The Harrisons seemed a little strange to

me from the beginning. They were from down Arkansas
way, and all looked as though made from the same mold.
Every one of them had coal black hair and brown eyes.
Each wore homespun pants and shirts that looked like they
were made from one bolt of cloth. This was the Harrison
clan, and from the looks of them they all ate from the same
pot at meal time too. A pot that was not nearly big enough
to feed all eighteen of them. They were hot tempered, and
skinny as rails. Even Janie, who was six months pregnant
didn't cast much of a shadow except around her middle.

There was Ma and Pa Harrison who were in their
late forties. Their three sons, Zeb, Jed, and Zeke. Their
wives Janie, Hanna and Beth all in their mid twenties, and
ten screaming brats that you couldn't tell one hardly from
the other.

They were kind of a stand-offish family that kept to
themselves, but it was plain to see that Pa Harrison was the
family monarch and his word was law right down to the
very youngest one. Zeb, being his oldest son, seemed to be
second in command and the women and children of the
family rarely spoke at all.

The wagon behind us was the Roberts family. They
were more like the people back home. Mr. Roberts was
taller than Pa, with receding brown hair and a thin mustache.
He was a friendly man with a ready smile and liked to be
called Bob. His wife Rebecca was surely Irish. She had long
red hair that hung to her waist in a braided pony tail, and
more freckles than you could count. She also had a wee bit
of an accent that left no denying her ancestry.

They had two children, Will who was eight and
Nancy, who was ten. Both had the bright red hair and
freckles of their mother, and the quick smile of their father.
They were farmers too, and like us, they had been wiped
out by the flood. Unfortunately, there wasn't enough of
their farm left to sell. I was glad they were right behind us.
Misty, now eleven, hadn't had a friend her own age in quite
some time, and on the long days ahead it would be nice to

have someone to talk to.

It took two weeks to get to Independence Missouri, but the road had been fairly good and the only rains we had were little more than a sprinkle. In the next few days as we started through Kansas the going wasn't quite so easy. By this time we were on a wagon trail instead of a road. The Prairie grass, green and up above my knees, looked like ripples on the water when the warm breeze blew up from the south.

We were in rolling prairie country, with one swell after another. On and on, each day seeming like the last. Sometimes we could tell we were on the right trail by the old ruts left in the mud of years gone by, and some times we just had to trust Jimmy, to know the way and to find us enough water to fill our barrels.

One evening as we were setting up camp Pa hobbled the horses as Misty and I went down to the creek bed to get wood for our evening fire. On days like this when we camped near a creek it was easy to get enough firewood, if you hurried. If you dilly dallied around and was one of the last to go looking for wood, you'd have to go quite a ways to find any. I would always try to get a little more than we needed so I could put some in the canvas sling Pa had rigged under the wagon. He had put it there so Misty and I could gather sticks and save them as we traveled. Later, as we got farther out into the plains we'd use buffalo chips, but as long as I could find wood for our cooking fires I was going to keep that sling plumb full.

When Misty and I came back from gathering firewood we saw Pa standing by one of the horses that was laying down. It was our mare that was due to foal at any time, so we dropped our wood by the fire pit and ran out to see what was wrong. When we got there she was breathing hard, and gasping for air.

"Is she going to be all right Pa?" Misty asked with a pale look on her face. She was always concerned about any creature in pain.

"I think so Misty, it's just time for her to have that colt," Pa reassured her with a smile and a gentle pat on the shoulder.

"Do you mean my colt Pa? The one you said would be mine."

"That's the one."

"Jeremy did you hear? Pa said I'm going to have my own horse."

With that Misty ran back to the wagon to tell Ma. They were a lot alike in that respect. Not only did they look alike with their long blond hair and sky blue eyes, but they both seemed to get so excited over things that Pa and I just took in stride. I mean if you have a mare that's going to foal, you get ready for it and be prepared to help if necessary, or stand back and smile if not. But not them, they just wait till the last minute and get all excited like it was a new member of the family being born.

Pa and I cut a couple of limbs off one of the trees down by the creek and used the wood sling from under the wagon to build a small lean-to over the mare because the clouds were building to rain.

I knew she was having a tough time of it by the way she was breathing and covered with sweat. Pa just said sometimes the first one comes hard and not to worry.

About an hour later it had started to rain and she was still struggling. Now even Pa began to worry that he might have to take the colt to keep from losing them both. All the sudden there was a clap of thunder, the mare squealed and out came the cutest little filly you ever saw. I don't know who was more relieved, the mare or Pa, but they were both doing better and began looking over the new colt, with three white stockings and a white star on her forehead.

Misty was at the wagon helping Ma with dinner and Pa went to get her. As she got there, the thunder rumbled again off to the west, and the little chestnut filly scrambled to her feet peeking around the canvas lean-to trying to see what was making that noise. Again the thunder rumbled, and she took a couple of wobbly steps toward the sound.

The mare grunted a little and lunged to her feet. With a soft nicker she called the little filly back to the small amount of shelter offered by the lean-to.

"Thunder!" Misty exclaimed, "I think I'll call her Thunder."

"You know she's going to be a lot of work, don't you?" Pa asked grinning, because he knew there was nothing in the world that Misty would rather do than to take care of her very own horse. "You're going to have to make a place in the back of the wagon for her to ride part of the time until she can keep up."

Misty spent half the night rearranging the wagon to make enough room for the new passenger. She was so excited that she couldn't sleep, and talked so much that nobody else could either.

And so it went for the next two weeks, Pa would put Thunder in the wagon to ride for a while, then he would take her out to walk by her mother. It seemed like no time at all until she could keep up, and Misty was with her every step of the way.

Chapter Three

We were almost halfway across Kansas before
the first real trouble on the trip. We had been traveling
across the rolling prairie for the last two weeks in hot
dry weather. For days at a time there wasn't even a
breeze. This was the most miserable traveling we had
done so far. It seemed every bug in the country could
smell the moisture in our sweaty clothes and they were
swarming us constantly. Tempers were short and small
disagreements turned quickly to heated arguments.

Only the Roberts family seemed unaffected by the
miserable conditions. Mr. Roberts drove the wagon while
his wife and children walked alongside singing songs from
a tattered old hymnal. The harder the going got, the
louder they sang, and each night they thanked God for the
wonderful day he had given them.

Finally one afternoon we came to a small river. It
wasn't much, but it was running clear and cool, and the
trees along the banks offered welcome shade. We stopped
early that night to give everyone a chance to bathe, and

wash some clothes.

The women went downstream through the trees, and the men went upstream. Tempers subsided quickly as the cool water washed away the miles. We splashed and played more than we washed, and it was good to hear laughter again. Pa and I were some of the first to arrive back at camp, and were putting together a fire, when Pa Harrison came in dragging his oldest grandson by the hair. The boy was kicking and screaming. He was only about thirteen years old, and shouted frantically as he tried to free himself, "I never Pa. I swear I never."

"Shut up Josh. I know what you was doin'," Pa Harrison said throwing the boy head long into the rear wheel of the wagon. He just laid there stunned while Pa Harrison grabbed a length of rope out of the wagon. He tied the boys hands to the top of the wheel and spread his feet tying them to the sides. As we watched in amazement, Pa Harrison went back to the wagon and brought out a long rawhide bullwhip. He tore the boys shirt open, stepped back, and struck with the whip tearing flesh down the length of his back.

Pa was on him in a flash, grabbing his wrist before he could strike a second time. "What do you think you're doin'?" Pa said between clenched teeth barely controlling his anger. "He can't deserve this kind of beating."

"He sneaked down river," Pa Harrison said, "spyin' on the women folk, he was."

"Did you see him do it?" Pa asked still holding tightly to Mr Harrison's wrist.

"Didn't have to, he came walkin' up the river with a big grin on his face, and I just knowed what he was about."

"You can't beat him like this, even if he did do it, and you aren't sure he did."

"I'll thank you to stay out of Harrison business," the man said as he hit Pa in the face with his left hand.

Pa wasn't expecting it and he landed hard on the

ground as Harrison struck with the whip again. The boy screamed as the whip once again tore at his flesh, and slipped into welcome unconsciousness. The old man was swinging the whip back for another strike when Pa hit him with a solid right to the kidney. Harrison grunted like a hog killed with a hammer, and went to his knees, clutching the small of his back barely able to breath. Pa figured it was over and went to untie the boy from the wagon. Harrison came to his feet swinging the whip once more, catching Pa around the middle. He screamed in shock and grabbed the end of the bullwhip. I had never seen Pa so mad. He started toward Harrison going hand over hand down the whip. The older man jerked hard trying to break Pa's hold on his only weapon, but he just kept coming.

Harrison was no match for Pa's strength. Pa wasn't real tall, just five foot nine, but he was wider in the shoulders than men much taller. He was strong and tough as nails from years of hard work, and right now he had a job that needed doing.

Pa stepped close and hit Harrison with a chopping right that made him buckle at the knees and stumble backward. He grabbed a handful of hair and smashed his fist into the man's nose, splattering blood everywhere, and sending him to the ground. Harrison came to his knees spitting out a tooth. He wiped the blood from his eyes with the back of his sleeve and dove at Pa's legs, only to catch a knee in the face. This time he was done as he rolled to his back gasping for breath. "Hold it," Zeb Harrison said, stepping around the wagon with a rifle in his hands.

Pa was in trouble but I didn't know what to do, and my feet felt like they were stuck to the ground. Zeb held his gun on Pa while old man Harrison tied his hands to the front wheel of the wagon.

"Now," growled Pa Harrison, "I'll learn ya to stay out of other folks affairs."

I felt my stomach turn over as Pa Harrison drew back the whip. He looked evil with his nose smashed flat, causing blood to run down his face and all over his shirt. Pa had knocked out one of his front teeth giving him a wicked grin, and I could tell he was going to enjoy this.

He struck like lightning, ripping Pa's shirt and the flesh on his back. Pa knew it was coming so he clenched his teeth against the bite of the whip. He willed himself not to cry out in pain, but a loud gasp escaped his lips.

Pa Harrison laughed as he drew back his whip. "Not so uppity now, John, are ya?" he laughed again as the whip tore more flesh. Pa was as strong as any man I had ever seen, but I didn't know how much more he could take. I started to yell for help, but it was as though someone was choking me. I had a lump in my throat and the words wouldn't come. I felt helpless and alone as I searched frantically for someone that could help.

That's when Jimmy came out of the trees moving low to the ground. He was as quiet as a ghost, and as fast as a panther. In seconds he had moved right up against Pa Harrison's back. In his right hand he held a colt pointed at Zeb, who didn't even know he was there yet. In his left hand was a fourteen inch Bowie knife with the razor sharp edge already starting a trickle of blood from old man Harrison's throat.

"Drop it," Jimmy said in a low even voice, leaving no doubt that he was serious.

Zeb swung the rifle, firing a quick round that went far wide of its mark, and Jimmy shot him where he stood. He fell back under the wagon clutching at his left shoulder and whimpering like a whipped pup. Pa Harrison dropped his whip, as he lost all heart to finish the fight.

Seeing his son writhing on the ground, Pa Harrison was completely subdued and Jimmy let him go. Zeb was breathing heavy but not hurt to where he wouldn't recover.

Jimmy stepped over to the wagon still holding a gun on the Harrison's, and used his Bowie knife to cut the ropes holding Pa and Josh to the wagon wheels.

"Out here," Jimmy said, "never figure it's over till it's over, and always watch your back. Especially with these clannish ones. I didn't figure to mix in with this as long as it was just family, and didn't get to serious, but by the time you stepped in I knew I better come a running, seein's how there's four of them and all."

"I appreciate your help Jimmy," Pa said. "I didn't figure to get mixed up in it either, but when I saw what he was doing to that kid I lost my temper. I just can't abide a man whipping the hide off a youngen, for any reason."

By this time everyone was running back to the wagons to see what the shooting was about. Some were straggling along still pulling on clothes as they came in.

Ma winced when she saw Pa's bloody shirt and turned plumb pale when she saw the boy laying stretched out on the ground.

"John," she said, "we've got to put something on that. Come to the wagon."

"I'm OK," Pa said, "see to the boy, I think he's hurt bad."

"I'll see to the both of you. Now come on, and some of you others bring the boy to our wagon."

"No! We'll take care of our own," shouted Pa Harrison glaring over his wounded son.

Ma just glared back at him, and then looked to the boy who was scared half to death. "I think you have done enough for him already. You, bring the boy to our wagon," she said pointing to a man in the front of the crowd.

With Ma in the wagon putting salve on their cuts, things calmed down a little while Jimmy explained the situation, to Mr. Reeves. He told how he had seen the whole thing from up the river, and how the old man had intended to whip the boy without mercy.

Mr. Reeves thought about it for a while then made up his mind. He went straight to Pa Harrison and said, "We are going to move your wagons up to the front of the train where I can keep an eye on you, and we'll be taking your guns and bullwhip too."

"No," Pa Harrison said, "you're not going to treat us like prisoners. We'll stay here. There's plenty of water and some good bottom land, and no one to mix in our business."

"Your choice," Mr. Reeves said, "but until we leave in the morning I'll have a guard watching you close."

"I'll be seein' you again Jimmy," Jed said, his voice shaking a little, "I got a score to settle for my brother Zeb."

Jimmy looked at him as calm as could be, "If I see you out on the prairie, away from your wagons, I'll figure you're hunting me, and I'll leave you to the buzzards. You can count on it." He turned his back and walked away like a man who had been threatened many times before, and had no time to waste worrying about the future.

As we were preparing to leave the next morning Pa Harrison came looking for the boy. "Where's Josh?" he said, almost in a casual manner, "I want the boy."

Pa was ready for him this time and he raised his rifle above the wagon seat where he was perched, leveling it at Pa Harrison's chest. "The boy stays," Pa stated flatly. "He says you'll kill him sure if he goes with you. I believe he's right."

"You can't take him just like that," Pa Harrison yelled "taint right."

"Yes we can," Mr. Reeves was talking now. He had come up behind Harrison. "We had a meeting last night and took a vote. It was unanimous. We'll keep the boy. He'll be well taken care of and he has a family ready to take him in as soon as he's well."

"You ain't heard the last of this Mr. Reeves," Pa Harrison sneered, "not by a long ways you ain't."

So we left with the whole Harrison clan staring at each of us as we passed. It was as if they were making sure they would know us all in days to come.

Chapter Four

Four days earlier and many miles to the west, a young Cheyenne boy in his fourteenth summer, was trying desperately to find his place among his people. He was the only son of Night Hawk, a powerful medicine man, who was said to have the ability to see glimpses of the future.

Night Hawk had named his son Runs with the Wind when he was a small boy, and he did his best to live up to the name. At fourteen, he was the fastest runner in the whole Cheyenne village. Runs with the Wind could match the skill of the warriors with a bow or lance, but his size continued to be a problem. He was sure he was cursed because the other boys his age were nearly a head taller, though not much stronger. Surely he had angered the spirits somehow and they were refusing to let him grow. He was sure that the only way to rid himself of this curse, was to go on a vision quest, to talk to the spirits and appease them anyway he could.

Night Hawk was proud of his son, yet he feared for his safety because of his size. Some boys never returned from their quest, and Night Hawk thought this may be true for Runs with the Wind. He had done his magic with the plants and smoke the night before in his medicine lodge and had talked to the spirits about Runs with the Wind and his quest. But the dream had been very confusing. Runs with the Wind was sitting on a small hill meditating with the spirits while all around him men were fighting. On one side of the hill Indians were trying to kill him and white men were protecting him, while on the other side of the hill white men tried to kill him and Indians were protecting him.

"Be careful my son," Night Hawk said as Runs with the Wind prepared to leave. "Remember the dream I have told to you. Know your friends with your heart, and your enemies with your knife."

Runs with the Wind nodded as he turned to walk away into the rising sun. He was dressed in only a loin cloth and moccasins. His straight black hair hung well below his shoulders, in a braid tied with a beaded leather strap. His copper skin glistened in the sun as it stretched over tight muscles that belied his size. He carried only a deer skin to sleep on, his hunting knife, a bow and a small quiver of arrows slung over his shoulder. He had two days supply of dried meat in a small pouch tied around his waist. He would eat part of it today, as he searched out a place to talk to the spirits. Then he would fast and meditate for three days, as his father had taught him, eating the rest on the return trip home.

The day passed quickly as Runs with the Wind walked through the trees and broken hills toward the east, his mind drifted off to his vision quest. What would it be like to talk to the spirits. Would you really leave your body and fly among the night fires of those who have gone before. Would you soar like an eagle above the prairie and be able to see all things clearly. Having gone on his vision quest he could participate in the Sun Dance ceremony at the summer gathering that would take place in the next moon. There were so many things to think about, so many things to remember.

He wondered, because of his size, would the people still consider him a boy when he returned, or would they see a young man and a warrior when he walked through camp. All these things were going through his mind as he crossed the small stream and started up the steep slope on the other side.

This hill was the tallest he had crossed all day and when he reached the rocky outcropping at the top, he stopped to gaze around. Across the valley below he could see a small herd of buffalo grazing peacefully. To the north a band of antelope were laying down with only their heads sticking up out of the grass to watch for any sign of danger.

As he watched, an eagle appeared from the east coming as straight toward him as an arrow shot. The great bird caught the up draft of the warm afternoon air soaring in a wide circle around the out cropping of rocks where he stood. It circled a second time closer to the ground. Again and again it circled, each time coming closer and closer, until it disappeared behind the rocks. Runs with the Wind waited for it to reappear on the other side but it didn't come out. It had simply vanished.

Suddenly he realized, what he had seen was no ordinary eagle, this was a spirit messenger. This was the place he was to stop. He had found it, without realizing this was what he had been looking for. It was perfect. He could feel the spirits in the animals, in the wind, and in the earth itself.

He began gathering sticks for his sacred fire. It would take a lot of wood to keep his little fire going for three days and three nights while he meditated. When satisfied that he had enough, he spread his deer skin out on the soft grass next to a huge rock that rose several times higher than his head. This was a good place he thought. Facing the rising sun in the morning and shaded from the heat of the afternoon. He was anxious to get started, but his father had warned him about rushing the spirits. If he tried to hurry things along the spirits would become angry and bring him no vision at all, or maybe even worse, they might bring him a vision of death. Yes, he thought, I must stay focused on my quest, and do everything just as my father has taught me.

He took the last of this days dried meat out of his pouch and slowly chewed a piece while he put together his small fire. Once the flame was strong enough to hold, he offered up prayers to the four directions, to the stars, and to earth mother herself. Then he placed the last of his dried meat in the flames as an offering to be carried to the spirits on the smoke. Now he could only wait.

He sat on the deer skin with his legs crossed and arms out stretched to the spirits above. He began chanting the vision prayer his father had taught him long ago. Over and over through the night he kept repeating the prayer. By morning he was hungry and exhausted, but these were the selfish thoughts of man that must be put aside if he was to achieve his vision. He concentrated on chanting louder and with more determination.

Finishing his morning prayers, Runs with the Wind searched the sky and the valley, for a sign of his coming vision. All day, and into the night he searched, to no avail. It must come, his heart was pure and his thoughts were only for the spirits. He opened his eyes to a bright morning sun. Exhilarated by the new feeling of awareness. His prayers had new meaning today, coming with a freshness he had never experienced. By late afternoon he was becoming weak and light headed. The vision was coming. His father had told him of these first signs. By dark he was exhausted and his chanting, though strong in his mind, was only mumbles on his lips. As the moon passed behind the rocks his eyes slid closed and he slipped into the world of spirits.

The vision started out pleasant enough with a new sun rising on a beautiful morning. Birds were singing and the world was at peace. He had become the great eagle, or at least he could see through the eyes of the magnificent bird. He watched the buffalo graze as a cow gently licked her new calf. Then it was dark, and a tall warrior from a tribe known to Runs with the Wind as Comanche, was standing over him with a wicked smile on his face. He tried to get up but the warrior knocked him down with a sharp blow from a war club. Runs with the Wind suddenly found himself in a vision where he was laying with his bloody face in the dirt and his hands and feet tightly bound. He struggled to get up and the big warrior kicked him in the ribs sending the air rushing out of his body.

Relax, he thought to himself after catching his breath I must not anger the spirits. Let the vision come, and he slipped back into his chanted prayer.

The sun was coming up again and the birds were singing. Yes it was going to be a good vision after all. As Runs with the Wind turned his head to the rising sun he saw the warrior again, only now there were two of them talking in a language he could not understand. As they turned toward him he realized this was not an ordinary vision. Some how, possibly because he was so small, he had taken his body as well as his spirit on his vision quest. This could be why the spirits were angry. Maybe this is what happened to those boys who never returned. Their bodies would go with the spirit on the quest and not be able to return. He prayed for the spirits to let the eagle, whom he was sure was his spirit animal, guide him safely through his vision.

As the two warriors approached, Runs with the Wind struggled to get up. He knew if he could just get his feet under him he could easily out distance the two warriors in this broken terrain. Something was wrong, his hands and feet wouldn't move.

The warriors dragged him to his feet and untied the rawhide strips around his ankles. Runs with the Wind was already planning his escape when the tall warrior slipped a loop of rawhide around his neck and tied the other end around his own wrist. Shoving him roughly they headed east. Runs with the Wind hadn't taken five steps when the tall warrior jerked hard on the leather thong bringing him down hard on his back choking and gasping for air. He laughed pulling Runs with the Wind to his feet by his hair and pushing him on down the trail.

Runs with the Wind figured it was a reminder of what would happen if he tried to get away. So he walked along the trail with his mind racing far ahead looking for a way out of this. As he walked alone in his thoughts the big warrior suddenly jerked hard on the leather thong again sending Runs with the Wind back to the ground choking once more. The two warriors both laughed and kicked at him as he rolled away trying to avoid the blows. He knew now why the two warriors had captured him. They needed a diversion from the boring endless travel through the dark side of the spirit world. They seemed to be venting their anger of some misfortune he knew nothing about, or maybe even worse, they were doing it because they enjoyed it. He didn't even want to think about that possibility. If that was the case, his beatings would get much worse.

Chapter Five

Josh was doing much better the next morning as we pulled away from the river, and he watched from the back of the wagon as his entire family glared at us. There was neither remorse nor happiness in him, it was simply one more event in his passage through life. As his eyes fell on his uncle Jed, he hid his face behind the canvas flap to keep from being seen. He knew Jed would be coming for him, and he was scared. This was one emotion he knew all to well. He didn't care that his father had been shot in the fight the day before, because he had always treated Josh more like a beast of burden than a son, beating him viciously when he failed to get enough work done or spoke out of turn. He would rather die than go back to the family, because Pa Harrison would be very harsh in delivering his punishment for this last indignity. He might even die, or worse yet, he might be severely crippled by the beating he knew was coming, leaving him with a more miserable existence than he had before. Either way he wasn't going back.

I rode in the wagon with Josh most of the first day and he told me how life had been for him back in Arkansas. How his family had lived on a small farm in the Ozark Mountains just south of the Missouri border. The farm had eventually became to small for their growing clan and Pa Harrison had taken his line of the family and gone to St. Louis to start over. It had been all right for a couple years, but then like most of the people on the wagon train, the floods had destroyed everything and they decided to go west.

"He's a cruel man," Josh said shivering as if he were suddenly cold. "I think he enjoys beating us, the way he always smiles and all."

"Well you won't have to worry about that any more," I assured him, "the Roberts said that they would take you in, and they're good people."

"We'll have to see about that, but it can't be as bad as living with Pa."

Mr. and Mrs. Roberts came into our camp that night to see how Josh was and to get to know him a little. At first Josh seemed a bit suspicious of their easy smiles and winning ways, but it wasn't long until they were getting along right well.

Mrs. Roberts measured him for size so she could make him a new shirt to replace the one Pa Harrison had torn off the day of the whipping. The one of Pa's that he was wearing now was so big he could turn around inside it. That was just as well for now with the cuts just starting to heal.

Over the next couple of days Will and Nancy Roberts came up to walk with us and talk to Josh who was still riding in the wagon.

"Jeremy," Josh asked one day, "why are those two always so cheerful? It don't seem natural."

"I think it's all that singin' and bible readin' their Ma does," I told him, "anyway I kinda like it."

"Yea, me to."

I knew then and there that he was going to do fine with the Roberts family. A kind word and gentle smiles were new to him but he was eating them up like watermelon at a summer picnic.

The fourth day after leaving the river Josh got out of the wagon and dropped back to walk with his new family. Except for the black hair and lack of freckles, he fit right in. By mid morning he had joined in with the singing and was smiling from ear to ear. It was hard to believe he had ever been a part of the Harrison clan, and I knew he could never be again.

Chapter Six

As the Harrison's hitched up their wagons there was a sullen tone in the air. Zeke was the hot head of the boys, and was ready to start trouble.

"When are we going after them Pa?" he asked reaching for his rifle, "the sooner the better, I say."

"Not yet," Pa Harrison calmly replied, "they'll be expecting us, and we can't afford for anyone else to get shot up right now. Besides we need to pick us out a piece of ground hereabouts and start putting a farm together."

"Are you just going to let them go Pa? Without gettin' even for Zeb?" Zeke was furious now.

"No, I ain't. But Jed'll take care of it when the time is right. You got too much temper. You'd just get yourself killed and do us no good to boot."

By noon Pa Harrison had found what he was looking for. It was a beautiful valley with the river running slow and deep on the west side. The east side of the valley was a flat bench well above the high water line just right for farming. At the north end of the valley the water ran fairly fast down the rapids, dropping suddenly over a small waterfall. This put the river high enough that they could easily dig a ditch to irrigate their crops.

Against the small hill on the east side where a clear spring seeped out of the rocks with water that was cool and sweet, stood a grove of cottonwoods that would provide welcome shade and shelter for their cabins.

Jed looked around with the eyes of a man who could see possibilities. This was a fine place to start over and raise his family. Only the dark thoughts of bringing Josh back to the wrath of Pa's whip could temper his enthusiasm for this place. Something had to be done. It was time for him and his brothers to raise their own families and for Pa to give advice rather than the whippings he seemed so prone to.

A few days later when the real work of building a farm had been started, Pa Harrison strode up to Jed like a man who had made a decision.

"Jed," he said, "tomorrow morning I want you to go after Josh and bring him back to me."

"Ain't it a little soon Pa?" he asked not really wanting to go at all.

"It's been five days now," Pa said, "and by the time you catch up with them without being seen, they'll figure we ain't comin'."

"OK Pa," Jed replied hesitantly, "but before I go, I gotta know you're not going to whip the hide off him when we get back."

Pa Harrison thought for a moment knowing Jed's soft spot for the kids and just how far he could be pushed, "I tell you what," he finally said, "when you get back we'll decide his punishment together. How's that?"

"Fair enough Pa," he replied, feeling only a little better about it. "I'll put my things together and get started at first light."

"One other thing boy," the smile had come back to Pa Harrison's lips. "I want Jimmy dead. Whatever it takes, he's gotta pay for what he done to Zeb."

"Sure Pa. Whatever you say."

Jed rode out the next morning at daylight with everything that had happened running through his mind, over and over. No matter how he thought about it there wasn't any sense in killing Jimmy. The more he thought about it the more he was sure that Jimmy could have killed Zeb if he wanted to, instead of just wounding him in the left shoulder. "I ain't gonna do it," he muttered to himself as he rode along, "I just ain't. I can tell Pa I did, and he'll never know the truth of it."

On and on he rode through the tall prairie grass, thinking about how to get Josh back without any trouble. He thought about how nice the farm would be when he took over his own family. If Pa wouldn't go along or tried to whip the kids anymore, he would take Janie and their two youngens, and find a farm of his own. This was beautiful country and he was sure he could find another place like the one they had now. And if Pa and Zeb were too rough on Josh, well, he'd take him along too.

For the first time in his life, Jed was feeling free of his fathers bonds, and he realized for the first time he really felt like his own man.

Following the wagon train was easy and as he rode along the trail Jed thought about how his new life would be. Twice he could have shot an antelope or deer but he just wasn't in the mood for killing. Life was going to be better now, he'd see to that, and there wasn't a thing Pa could do to stop it.

Chapter Seven

Since we had left the Harrison clan, three days earlier, Jimmy had been riding our back trail in the afternoon to make sure we weren't being followed. On the fourth afternoon as he was headed out he stopped long enough to tell us about the creek up ahead where we would camp and be able to get fresh water that night.

As he rode off Ma looked wistfully up along the trail we were taking. "It'll be nice to have fresh water," she said brushing a loose strand of hair from her sweat stained face. "To bad we don't have any fresh meat to go with it. I'm so tired of chewing dried meat and hard tack."

Pa just grinned as he looked over at Ma riding on the wagon seat beside him. He knew she had a taste for fresh venison, and it had been a while since we'd had any. There wasn't anything he wouldn't do for her.

"I'll talk to Mr. Reeves," Pa said still grinning, "maybe Bob and I can ride ahead and catch a deer or two by the creek."

He climbed off the wagon and untied Star, looping

the lead rope around the horse's nose making a crude bridle. Swinging aboard, he trotted off toward the front of the slow moving wagon train. Pa was never really comfortable riding bareback and you could see it now. Star's stiff legged trot and high withers made for pretty rough going.

When we came up on Pa a few minutes later he was standing by the trail waiting.

"Jeremy," Pa said, "climb in back and hand down the saddles. We'll need to barrow Renegade too, if you don't mind."

"Sure Pa," I yelled as I made my way back through the wagon.

As I handed down the gear, Pa and Mr. Roberts carried it to the side of the trail so they could saddle the horses without interfering with the trains progress. I handed down his rifle wishing I could go along.

"Good luck Pa," I shouted as we left them behind in the slowly rising dust.

Once they were saddled up, they rode off at a gallop putting the train as far behind as they could. I knew Pa would get something, for he rarely came back empty handed. He was an excellent shot and had learned to hunt sneaking through the wooded hills of southern Missouri when he wasn't much older than me.

As they came to the crest of a ridge they could see the tops of the trees marking the progress of the little creek winding it's way below.

"Hold up," Pa said wetting his finger and holding it slightly above his head, "the wind is coming from the south, not much, but a little, lets go down that little side draw there to the north. We can leave the horses there and work down stream on foot."

"Sounds good to me," Bob said swinging his horse to the North. "Let's get to it."

They tied their horses in the mouth of the draw near the creek where the trees would shade them and the rustle of the leaves would help cover any sounds they made.   Then working slowly they started downstream, making their way from one tree to the next.   Always staying in the shadows careful not to step on any twigs. After a short distance Mr. Roberts froze and motioned for Pa to stop too.

"Deer?" Pa asked.

"No," Bob replied still straining to hear, "I heard a voice."

"You sure?" Pa whispered looking more intently into the trees ahead.

"Yea, I'm sure, but I couldn't make out any words."

Quietly they waited straining to hear every sound beyond the chirping of birds and gentle rustling of leaves.

"There it is again.   Did you hear it?" Bob asked looking almost straight ahead.

"I did, but it ain't no white man," Pa replied, making sure his gun was fully loaded.

"We better get back and warn the others," Bob said with a worried look on his face.   He too was counting the extra cartridges in his pocket.

"I think we better take a look Bob.   We need to know what we're up against.   Besides if we get into trouble these two Henry repeaters will make enough noise that they'll know we ain't deer hunting."

With that they started working downstream again taking almost thirty minutes to cover the hundred yards or so to get to a good vantage point.

They watched as two braves argued while a young boy lay on the ground.   He was so still they would have thought him sleeping if it were not for the loud argument going on only a few feet from him.

Suddenly, the tallest brave dropped to his knees and pulled the young boys head back exposing his throat. Slowly he drew out his knife and with a cruel grin he laid the blade along the boys throat, teasing the flesh with the razor sharp edge causing droplets of blood to form from one ear to the other.

"We've got to do something," Bob said looking all around to see if this was all of the Indians, or if there were more hidden in the trees.

Satisfied there were only two Pa said, "I know we do. When I say now you shoot the one standing, and make it count. I'll take the one holding the boy." As Pa squeezed the trigger he was sure this was the most important shot he had ever made. It would have to be, to keep the warrior from slitting the boy's throat.

The whole train heard the shots and we could already smell the fresh venison roasting over an open fire. As we topped over the ridge we saw Pa riding up to Mr. Reeves at the head of the train. They talked for a moment and then both men raced off toward the creek.

When we got closer Mr. Reeves came riding back out to tell us where to circle the wagons near a small clearing. As we were making camp Jimmy rode up and Mr. Reeves called out to him. "Jimmy, come here," saying the words as calmly as possible trying not to alarm everyone.

Jimmy went over to the trees where Mr. Reeves, Pa, and Mr. Roberts were talking. After a moment of explanation Jimmy stood there, just shaking his head. "John, I'll be danged if you don't get us into more trouble with kids that ain't no concern of yours," Jimmy exclaimed, searching the horizon for any sign of danger.

Pa looked Jimmy square in the face, "I couldn't let them torture him any more. Look how badly he's been beaten already," and he bent down to check the boys condition one more time.

"I understand that John, but it's like I told you," Jimmy said seriously, "this is a hard land with hard choices. You better start making the right ones. Those two are Comanche. Probably scouts for a large hunting party. Their friends will surely follow them here. Could be anytime."

"What do we do then?" Mr. Roberts asked, thinking maybe it was a mistake to interfere with the Indians afteall.

"Fight," was Jimmy's only reply.

"Wait a minute," Pa said, "I've got an idea. let's give them a good christian burial."

"That won't stop them Indians from taking our scalps or wanting revenge," Mr Reeves scowled, not at all sure what to do about the situation.

"It might if they think we're burying one of our own," Pa said as he could see the plan taking shape.

Jimmy smiled as he replied, "Put 'em both in one hole and put up a cross, it just might work John."

Pa and Mr. Roberts put the Indian boy in our wagon along with a bow, some arrows in a quiver and a hunting knife. "Hide these Cheryl, we'll give them to him later, if he's friendly. He'll need them to get back home, wherever that is."

They returned to the trees and started digging a grave in a small clearing. It was just after sundown and they were putting up the cross when the Comanche hunting party came over the rise. There must have been ten of them in all. They stopped a short ways from the camp and two came in alone giving the hand sign for parley.

"They want to talk," Jimmy said walking out to meet them.

Pa went too, figuring it was because of him that they were in this spot. He knew he couldn't do any of the talking but if trouble started, at least he'd be there with Jimmy.

As they talked in signs and the Comanche language, we couldn't understand a thing they were saying. We could tell it was getting heated by the sharp gestures and loud voices. Suddenly the leader said something with a finality in his voice and pushed past Jimmy heading for the grave. Jimmy made a loud reply, laughed, and then repeated it again.

The Comanche leader stopped and whirled to look Jimmy square in the eyes, as if trying to read the truth.

Then letting out a squeal he left at a run. As he reached the rest of the hunting party, he spoke rapidly pointing at the gravesite. Soon all of the Indians were racing back over the ridge from which they had come.

"What was all that about?" Pa asked, with a quizzical look on his face. "He looked like he'd seen a ghost."

"He wanted to look in the grave," Jimmy replied evenly, "I told him to go ahead, 'cause a man that dies of smallpox doesn't care who looks at him."

Still a little uneasy about the close call, they grinned at each other knowing that Jimmy's quick thinking had saved them all.

"They might be gone for good," Jimmy said not really believing it. "But we better stand watch tonight, just in case they come back. Since you boys started this hoo-raw, you and Bob can take the first two turns. I'm gonna get some sleep, it's going to be a long night."

Chapter Eight

The vision was becoming clear again. Runs with the Wind found himself in a strange lodge, the likes of which he had never seen before. It wasn't a tepee because the top was rounded with one side open. The bottom and sides were all made of wood, and it was packed full of strange things. But the strangest thing of all was, it was moving. Runs with the Wind struggled to raise his head for a look around. Pain racked his body from the effort and dizziness overtook him. He managed a quick look, then collapsed back to the strangely colored robes. He tried to lay very still as he thought about the strange things he saw. There were many more lodges behind him, being pulled along by horses. There were also strange sounds and smells coming from all around him.

Runs with the Wind had never heard of such a vision as this, and felt that it must be of great importance. Surely the Spirits had powers greater than he imagined. At least they had untied him and his arms and legs were free. As he tried to move, he found that every part of his body hurt so bad that it was making him sick to his stomach.

Yes, he remembered now. It was the evil spirits that had captured him first when his vision had only begun. They had beaten him without mercy until he could remember nothing. Now he was here resting, as comfortable as possible for the condition he was in.

Somehow he had escaped or been taken away by the protecting spirits of the Cheyenne. That must be it, these were the protecting spirits, that's why their lodges moved. "They must be taking me home," his words were barely more than a whisper as he gazed around.

Suddenly a little spirit peeked over the side of the lodge through the opening in the back. It was a girl spirit with hair the color of the sun and eyes like the sky. He couldn't understand her words but her voice was gentle and soothing to listen to. As she laid a hand on his fevered forehead, the little Sun Spirit's touch was as soft as a well tanned rabbit fur, and he forgot the pain tormenting his body. Runs with the Wind raised a hand to touch the little spirit and she vanished. He could no longer see her but he could hear her talking to the other spirits in strange and magical tones. Why had the little spirit left him. Maybe he shouldn't have tried to touch her that way. But she was such a pleasure to look at, and to be so close, how could he not try.

"Pa he's awake," cried Misty running to the front of the wagon.

Pa quickly handed the reins over to Ma and as he leaped from the wagon seat he told me to go find Jimmy. It was almost time for the noon stop and I knew Jimmy would be close by. I grabbed Renegade's lead rope and swung to his back. Galloping to the lead wagon, I found Jimmy talking to Mr. Reeves. When we got back to the wagon, Pa was sitting in the back checking the injuries of a wide eyed Indian boy.

"Didn't think he'd set still for that," Jimmy said. You could almost see his grin peeking out from under his drooping mustache.

"See if you can find out anything Jimmy. What his name is, where he came from, anything."

Jimmy started off with the sign language that all plains Indians seemed to know, and the boy eagerly responded telling Jimmy he was a Cheyenne warrior on his vision quest. Realizing this Jimmy quickly broke into the native tongue that seemed to flow so smoothly off his lips. They talked for several minutes while Pa and I waited eagerly.

Finally they stopped and Jimmy began to tell us his story. "His name is Runs with the Wind, and he was on a vision quest when two evil warrior spirits captured him. He thinks he's still in his vision and we're the protector spirits that are taking him home."

"Did you tell him we are just white folks that want to help him?" Pa asked.

"I tried, but he insists we're spirits."

"Tell him about how we saved him from the Comanche," Pa said, "maybe he'll believe you then."

So Jimmy set to explaining how Pa and Mr. Roberts had come upon him and his captors. Runs with the Wind especially liked the part where we had buried the Comanche's in the ground and scared the others away with the story of small pox. He laughed, thinking Cheyenne warriors would not be so easily fooled, and the pain shot through his badly bruised ribs like fire. He tried not to show the pain so we all pretended not to see it.

How he wished that he had paid more attention when his father tried to teach him the white mans language. At the time it seemed like a wasted effort, when he was trying to master the skills of a warrior, to waste his energy on the words of people he had never seen.

That day and the next Misty rode in the wagon with Runs with the Wind. He was fascinated with her long blond hair and quick smile but more importantly she was teaching him the white mans words. Runs with the Wind learned quickly and in two days had memorized the words for most everything in the wagon train. He wasn't conversational, but I was surprised at how much he had absorbed in such a short time.

By the third morning he had taken about as much laying around as any man could take and decided to get out and walk. It was amazing how fast he was recovering from such a beating. He showed almost no pain, with his concentration focused on learning.

Misty and I walked with him and she talked constantly showing him flowers and rocks, plants and trees, everything along the trail. When she introduced him to Thunder he made a fine show of what a wonderful horse it was, and Misty's eyes lit up with pride.

Whether intentional or not, Runs with the Wind was teaching us the Cheyenne words at the same time. The sounds felt strange in my mouth and we had trouble forming the words at first. He would laugh softly and keep repeating them until he was satisfied with the results.

By late afternoon his muscles had loosened up from the walking and the cool breeze was making him restless. He decided to do what he did best, and that was to run. He ran along the wagon train toward the front and I did my best to keep up. By the time we got back to our wagon I was panting hard and my throat was burning dry. I couldn't keep up with the fast pace, and he didn't seem to be half trying. I went to the water barrel and started gulping it down. Runs with the Wind took the ladle from my hand saying the Cheyenne word for no. Still holding the ladle in his hand he took a mouthful of water and raced away from the wagon. This time he cut loose and ran a hundred yards or so out into the prairie and back. I was stunned, even Renegade would have a hard time keeping up in a short race. As he reached the wagon he spit the water at my feet and handed me the ladle. This must be a challenge I thought as I dipped up the water. I took a mouthful and started running. Almost immediately I knew what Runs with the Wind was trying to teach me. I had to breath through my nose instead of my mouth. As I returned to the wagon I realized that my throat and lungs weren't burning the way they had before. I spit the water out unceremoniously drenching his feet. We both laughed as he placed a strong hand on my shoulder using the English word, "Good."

The next afternoon as we walked to the top of a rise we could see some broken hills to the west of us. Runs with the Wind stopped and looked hard at the hills and said very slowly, "My Pa, hills."

"What?" Misty asked.

"My Pa! Hills," he repeated pointing to the horizon.

"That must be where he lives. We better tell Pa," I said.

That night when I told Pa that we were getting close to his home, he went to the wagon and brought back the bow, quiver of arrows, and hunting knife that he had taken from the Comanche. As Pa handed them over, Runs with the Wind's eyes lit up like a kid at Christmas. What a trophy this would be, to return from his vision quest with a Comanche warrior's weapons. Surely the Spirits must be happy with him now, to show him such favor.

When we started out the next morning the hills were little more than a days travel away, and Runs with the Wind became more serious about learning. As we walked along I knew he would be leaving us soon. It was strange though, I kinda hated to see him go.

Chapter Nine

It had been seven days since the wagon train had left the Harrisons behind and Jed was coming up on them fast. Riding alone on horseback he could cover the miles much faster than the slow moving wagons.

Late the first evening he had a close call with disaster almost riding right into a large band of Comanches. He had been thinking about the changes in his life and was not paying attention to his surroundings.

Starting over the rise he caught a glimpse of movement in the trees near the creek below. Thinking it might be Jimmy waiting in the brush, he dismounted quickly, and ground hitched his horse out of sight. Hoping he hadn't been seen, as only his head had been above the horizon, he crawled to the crest to have a better look. He lay there peering through the grass with the sun beating down on his back for what seemed like hours, but this was no time to hurry. As he watched the trees where the movement had been, a large Comanche warrior stepped into view. He wasn't painted for war, but he was pretty intent on tracking something or someone. The warrior's eyes searched the ground at his feet trying to work out the trail. There were moccasin prints here and there but he was sure they were not the prints of his two missing companions. He turned sharply and walking back into the trees only to return several minutes later followed by more warriors. Together they studied the prints. The people of the wagon train must have been very busy, to have made so many prints over such a large area. It was impossible to follow the trail through there.

Jed watched as the Indians spread out searching for tracks. The large warrior he had seen first, started up the ridge toward him. He glanced around to find no cover, save the waving prairie grass that would never conceal him and his horse. To the north, the ridge turned slightly to the west, not much but maybe enough to let him escape as the warriors come over the crest. If he was careful he could manage to slip over the top and follow the little draw down to the creek, then work upstream until he found enough cover to get out of the little valley.

He had just rounded the little break in the ridge, when the large Comanche warrior came over the crest, far ahead of the others. As he watched, an empty feeling welled up in the pit of his stomach. He hadn't had time to cover the trail, and the warrior was headed straight for it.

The Comanche stopped abruptly, when he came across the freshly made tracks of a white mans horse. The shoes were new and made unmistakable prints in the dry prairie grass and hard packed soil, but it was hard to tell just how fresh they were. He squatted, studying the tracks carefully before looking up to stare in the direction Jed had gone. He had taken only a dozen steps, when he stopped again to look over the rolling landscape. Jed knew that he was trying to decide whether or not to follow the tracks. At that moment the huge Comanche's eyes locked on the exact spot where Jed was hiding. The warrior, also, had figured out that a man could hide around that little bend.

As he squatted to study the tracks with renewed interest, Jed slowly inched his way back to his horse. He led the animal as quietly as possible, to a small saddle where the ravine started down the other side of the ridge. The grass was sparse here with waist high brush and dogwood running down both sides of the draw. The bottom was mostly sand and loose soil leaving clear sign of any passage. Down he went through the sandy soil leading his horse to the trees, where he tied him well out of sight. Circling around he started back up the ravine parallel to the trail that had been made while coming down. When he came to a spot where his first trail could be plainly seen going well into the trees he stopped. Then crawled toward the center of the draw to a place that was well concealed from view by the thick brush.

The Comanche brave came slowly over the crest, studying the trail carefully. Since the man had hidden in the grass around that little bend and then had carefully lead his horse away, he was sure the white man had been watching him. This might be what had happened to his two companions. He could see the tracks below leading into the trees and watched them closely as he continued on his way.

Jed let him take two painfully slow steps, past the point where he lay concealed, before coming silently off the ground. With the agility of much practice the ambush was completed with one quick swing of the rifle. The barrel caught the brave just above the left ear dropping him in an unconscious heap. After dragging him into the brush Jed covered the tracks of the struggle as best he could and hurried back to his horse.

He rode along the creek until he found a place to get out undetected, and once over the rise he headed southwest at a lope. Jed was sure he had to reach the wagon train soon or the Comanches would be on him. It wouldn't be long before they discovered their missing friend and followed the trail he wasn't trying to hide.

By the next afternoon, with no sign of pursuit, he began to relax. He could see the dust of the wagons as they moved along. His horse was nearly spent and he needed to find a place to rest. He had ridden hard through the night afraid to stop with the Comanche hunting party behind him.

The terrain was changing some here. There were broken hills and more trees. The prairie grass was becoming more and more sparse with each passing mile. Jed chose a spot on the east slope of a small hill, covered with scattered trees, where he could rest while he watched his back trail. He could easily catch up with the wagon train during the night and take Josh without too much trouble. Right now he and his horse needed rest.

At sundown Jed started after the wagon train. As he rode through the pale moonlight he put together a plan. His horse was done in and wouldn't be able to handle the rigorous trip back across the plains. He was going to have to travel fast because Jimmy would chase him for a day or so, but he couldn't be away from the wagon train any longer than that. Then there was the Comanches to think about. Surely they were going to be in a nasty mood.

It was just after midnight when he reached the camping spot of the wagon train. He circled slowly in the last of the pale moonlight finding the wagon he was looking for. He waited until the moon went down leaving nothing but the light of the stars to betray his presence.

Jed worked in slowly leading his exhausted horse right up to Renegade, who paid little attention to the man with the familiar scent. Working quietly he hobbled his horse and took off the saddle. Walking to Renegade he laid a gentle hand on his withers and stroked his back. When he was sure that Renegade wouldn't put up a fuss he quietly put the saddle on his back and cinched it up tight. Renegade was big and powerful, like his own horse, plenty strong enough to carry him and Josh both. He hated to take the horse knowing it belonged to me, but he had no choice. At least he was leaving an excellent horse in trade. Jed figured after a few days I would recognize the quality of the new horse, and maybe forgive him for the swap in the night.

Jimmy felt the call of nature and could no longer ignore it. As much as he hated to, he was going to have to get up to take care of the problem. The moon had just gone down and he hated to tromp around in the dark barefooted, so he fumbled around in the dark finding only one moccasin. Well at least one foot is protected, he thought, stumbling over a rock. Cursing under his breath, he decided this would have to be far enough. Just as he started to undo his pants he caught a glimpse of movement over by some of the horses. It could have been a man, or maybe just his imagination. For long seconds Jimmy watched. There it was again. The man left the horses, heading for the wagons. He seemed to be sneaking.

Jed slid quietly between the wagons until he found what he was looking for. Recognizing the wagon he peered in back. There was Josh, sleeping like a baby. Tucked in all cozy and warm with nothing but the top of his head sticking out of the handmade quilt. This was going to have to be done fast. Timing was everything now. Reaching into the wagon he clamped a hand over the boys mouth as he grabbed a shoulder and pulled. The young boy came out of the wagon easily and without much struggle. "This is going to be easier than I thought," he said to himself, as the young Cheyenne brave buried a knife in his heart.

Jed fell to the ground with a light thud. Runs with the Wind couldn't believe he had killed a white man. Frantically he reached in the wagon and grabbed the bow and quiver of arrows, thanking the spirits that had convinced John to save them. Turning abruptly he ran into the night almost colliding with Jimmy.

"Hello," Jimmy said, startled to see the young Cheyenne. Runs with the Wind said nothing and kept going into the darkness.

That's strange, Jimmy thought as he continued to look for the other man. As he stepped around the back of our wagon his foot bumped into something soft. Realizing it was a man he bent down to find the warm, wet trickle of blood over the heart.

"Runs with the Wind!" he called loudly in Cheyenne, "come back."

The silence of the camp was broken and people were poking their heads out of the wagons or running up to see what was the matter.

Runs with the Wind ran to the horses to make his escape. Finding Renegade saddled and ready to go, he swung up thanking his eagle spirit once more for his good fortune. Turning to leave he called out in Cheyenne, "Good bye Brother of the Wind, thanks for the horse, and take care of the little Sun Spirit." Then he was gone into the night.

"What's going on?" Pa demanded as he climbed out of the wagon.

"Jed came for Josh and got Runs with the Wind instead," Jimmy said piecing the story together. "Now Runs with the Wind is scared because he killed a white man, so he took Renegade and left. Probably headed home."

"He took Renegade?" I said choking on the words.

"Yes, and he yelled a message for you as he left."

"What."

"He said, good bye Brother of the Wind thanks for the horse, and take care of the little Sun Spirit. He really liked you two, I think."

"Yea, he calls me brother, but he steals my horse." I was so mad I cursed the day Pa saved him.

Some of the other men took care of Jed's body and the rest of us went back to bed. There was nothing we could do about Runs with the Wind. We couldn't track him in the dark and by morning he would have a long head start.

I tossed and turned all night unable to sleep, because the more I thought about it the madder I got.

The next morning as we were preparing to leave Jimmy came up to me leading a strange horse. "This was Jed's horse, now she's yours," he said handing me the reins.

She was a big bay, well bred and powerful. Under other circumstances I would have been proud to have her, but right then all I could think of was Renegade.

"Saddle her up, and try her out," Jimmy said hoping to make me feel better.

"Good idea," Pa said seeing his intentions.

Reluctantly I got out my saddle and tried it on her for size. It was perfect and I was riding along the wagons as we pulled out. I rode quietly for a while, then venting my anger I kicked her hard in the ribs with my heals. She leaped forward almost unseating me and was instantly running. In no time we caught up with the front of the wagon train. Jerking hard on the reins we wheeled around and raced back the way we came. As I passed our wagon Pa waved me on with a smile on his face. I had to admit, she sure could run.

Chapter Ten

Reaching the back of the wagon train, I couldn't make myself stop. On and on we ran until I reached the spot where we had camped the night before. Within minutes I found the tracks of Renegade, where he broke into a run, headed northeast. I followed for a ways and his trail stayed constantly going in the same direction. Suddenly I found myself following at a dead run. "We can catch him," I said, patting the horse on the neck. "When he realizes no one is chasing him he'll slow down. I can trade horses and be back to the wagon train before the evening stop."

I was young and my thoughts were only of retrieving my horse, never stopping to think about the possible dangers involved or how my folks would feel.

By noon I was almost ready to give up. I was going to look over one more rise, and if I couldn't see him by then I was going to head back. As my horse topped out we stopped to stare off to the north, and I couldn't believe my luck. Runs with the Wind was coming straight toward me at a dead run, bringing back my horse. That's when I noticed the band of Comanches that were chasing him. They were maybe a mile back but coming hard.

Renegade ran right past me as I turned to follow.

"Jeremy, come!" Runs with the Wind yelled as he passed me, his english better than I remembered it.

So I followed him, winding through the broken hills. Runs with the Wind sure knew what he was doing. We stayed mostly on hard ground that would not give away our trail so easily, and we changed directions often to confuse them. We had strong horses so we used rough ground to tire their mounts. All of their horses were carrying double our weight and that would help over the long run.

I was scared and my life depended on the warrior skills of Runs with the Wind. I was glad now that he called me brother.

We raced along the broken ground stopping when we had a long view of our back trail to get down and let the horses rest. After a while they didn't show up on one of our stops and we thought maybe we had lost them for the time being. Runs with the Wind headed west, and I had no choice but to follow. I was completely lost.

Chapter Eleven

Ma looked toward the back of the wagon train, and then at Pa, with a worried expression on her face, "I haven't seen Jeremy for quite awhile. You don't think he would go after his horse, do you?"

Pa had been worried about the same thing, and having it said out loud made his fears even stronger. "I'll go and see," he said pulling the wagon to a stop.

He saddled Star and shoved his rifle in the boot. "He can't have gone far, it's only been about an hour. Stay with the train and we'll catch up later."

"I'm scared John, he's only fourteen."

"Don't worry, he's got a good head on his shoulders. After he runs out his anger he'll turn around and I'll probably meet him coming back."

"Just hurry John, find him soon."

Pa understood how I felt, but by the time he had been on the trail a couple hours he was mad enough to give me a whipping suitable for the Harrison clan.

Star was fresher than the horse I was on so Pa was

able to gain ground slowly. Shortly after noon we were only a mile apart but we never saw him. Runs with the Wind wouldn't know for sometime to come that Pa was saving his life again, as well as mine.

Pa saw us though. He watched as we ran our horses to the top of the hill and climbed off hiding in the trees. He was trying to figure out what was going on when he heard a ...swish... followed by a thud... He felt something tug at his leg. Pain shot through him like a hot knife. He looked down to see a Comanche arrow protruding from his thigh. The stone point had gone clear through the muscle and lodged in the saddle under the swell. Jerking the reins he headed back to the wagon train kicking his horse in the ribs and yelling for Star to run faster.

As Star leaped into motion the arrow shaft broke between his leg and the saddle sending shock waves of pain through his leg. With every stride of the powerful horse the pain in his leg grew more intense.

The Comanche that had shot the arrow let out a blood curdling war whoop and began the chase. The other warriors sensing the heat of battle joined in.

They were close at first but Star was up to the run. The Comanches had been chasing Jed for a whole day before they chased us, and now they forced their already tired mounts into another hard run. This time the quarry was in sight and already wounded, so they pursued relentlessly.

By the time he could see the wagons, Pa was having trouble staying in the saddle, and the Comanches seemed a little closer. Was he faltering, he thought, had he slowed his pace without knowing. It was hard to tell, but it was becoming clear that he wasn't going to make it without some help.

Pulling his Henry repeater out of the boot he held it in his right hand and cradled it in the crook of his left arm as he continued to keep one hand on the saddle horn. He knew if he let go with his left hand he couldn't stay seated very long. Firing aimlessly across his saddle, his shots fell harmlessly across the plains far from his attackers. It slowed the pursuit for only seconds adding a few more yards of precious ground to his lead.

The Comanches soon realized this was a call for help and that the shots were being fired in a different direction. The already lathered ponies pulled harder still to the demands of their riders and the gap began to close.

"Indians," Bob yelled, remembering what John had said about the Henry rifle.

He pulled his wagon to an abrupt stop in the middle of the trail. He jumped from the seat with his rifle in hand and took off on foot toward the unsteady rider coming from the north. Jimmy and two other men caught up to him on horseback as he dropped into a buffalo wallow for protection. "Come on John, one more little rise and you're home free," he whispered almost under his breath.

John came over the ridge laying across the saddle horn with his left arm wrapped tightly around Star's neck. His right hand clung to the Henry that flopped against Star's side as he ran.

Jimmy caught Star's reins as he neared the buffalo wallow, and brought him to a stop at the edge. Pa fell from the saddle. He lay sprawled on the ground, exhausted from the long chase, with the arrow shaft still protruding from his leg.

Star was heaving heavily trying to get enough air into his burning lungs. His body covered with white foamy lather. He stood trembling as Jimmy removed the saddle to ease his burden. On his right hip was a long cut barely separating the hide, caused by a second arrow that went unnoticed at the time. Only Star's quick response to the reins had kept the arrow from piercing his heart, leaving his rider to face certain death. Instead the arrow had ripped along his hip as he made an abrupt turn.

The Comanche warriors had come to a halt still

some distance away, and seemed to be watching something off to the west with great interest. Jimmy's eyes scanned the area for several minutes before he saw what had caught their attention. It was a large Cheyenne hunting party that had been drawn over the far ridge by the rapidly fired shots.

The Comanches were greatly out numbered, and shortly decided to head back toward the east in a hasty retreat. The hunting party followed along to make sure they knew they were not welcome in the Cheyenne summer hunting grounds. We don't know how far they followed the Comanche, but that was the last we saw of them.

Chapter Twelve

Runs with the Wind and I waited on the hill watching our back trail. The Comanche never came. I couldn't believe how lucky we were that they had lost our trail. As we prepared to leave I grabbed Renegade's reins and started to climb on. Runs with the Wind jerked the reins out of my hand, and pointed to the other horse. He jumped onto Renegade's saddle and waited. I couldn't believe he was going to keep my horse. Being Cheyenne, he felt that since he had stolen my horse fair and square it was now his, and he wasn't about to give it up. We would see about that later, right now was not the time to fight over who rode which horse. Runs with the Wind smiled broadly as I climbed into the saddle.

"Well," I said begrudgingly, "I guess I can always call you Lady Renegade."

Runs with the Wind sat with his back straight, his chest puffed up, and a large smile on his face. He looked over at me and said, "Good! Renegade," pointing to his horse, "Lady Renegade," pointing to mine. Then he had the nerve to say, "Go now. Men lead," as he swung my horse around and left me sitting there on Lady Renegade.

I was so mad I didn't know what to do, but I had no choice in the matter, so I followed him not knowing where we were headed.

As we traveled west I didn't know what to do. I was sure Pa was out looking for me by now. He might even run into the Comanches as we had. I wanted to just ride away and go back to the wagon train, but I had no idea where it was, or if the Comanche were still behind us. I was afraid to go on, and more afraid not to.

The hills were getting larger all the time and just before dark I saw the tops of some blue mountains far to the west with traces of what looked like snow on the tops.

After spending the night sleeping on a damp saddle blanket, with no fire to give away our position, I woke up stiff and sore. We had no food or water, and though I was hungry, thirst was my major concern. I turned to wake Runs with the Wind, and he was gone! I looked around frantically. Nothing. I threw the saddle on Lady Renegade and started following his trail. It led up a small canyon to the north with several large cottonwood trees, a half mile away, towering over the more common junipers that stood all around. That must be it. With that small stand of cottonwood trees there must be a spring, or at least a seep. He was looking for water.

A hundred yards from the trees I heard a limb snap in the crisp air of the quiet morning. I could hear Renegade snorting violently as he stomped and kicked in the brush. I started to spur my horse ahead and was stopped by the deep voice of a man. A white man.

"Down boy, calm down or I'll use that stick on you too," I heard him say.

Leaping from my horse, I tied her securely to a tree and ran ahead on foot. As I got to the patch of cottonwoods I saw a man in buckskins with a long scraggly beard standing over Runs with the Wind. He held a limb as big as my arm in his right hand, and Renegade's reins in the other. Runs with the Wind was pushing himself up off the ground, holding his head with his left hand. As the man raised the club for a final blow I leaped to his back wrapping my right arm around his neck in a choke hold. He dropped the club and Renegade's reins as he grabbed me by the hair. He pulled and jerked flipping me over his shoulder into the brush. The mountain man started toward me with a wild eyed expression on his face. Runs with the Wind grabbed his legs from behind locking his arms around the ankles. The man tried to break his hold and Runs with the Wind sank his teeth into the buckskin leggings just below the knee.

"Aaaaa!" The mountain man screamed, grabbing Runs with the Wind by his loin cloth and his long black braid.

With his attention off me, I grabbed the club he had dropped. To late the mountain man remembered there were two of us, turning his head back to me, in time to catch the club right between the eyes. He flew backwards landing in the dirt by the little seep. He scrambled to his feet, clutching the stick as I swung again. Runs with the Wind picked up a rock the size of his head, and as we struggled for control of the club, he smashed the rock down on the closest moccasin.

"Aaaaa!" The mountain man screamed again letting go of the club and diving for Runs with the Wind, who was still on his hands and knees.

Striking down with the club, I hit him at the base of the skull. He landed solidly, dead weight, squarely on top of Runs with the Wind, where I left him.

I got on Renegade and rode back to the tree where Lady Renegade waited patiently. Leading her, I rode back to the seep. Runs with the Wind was drinking from the spring and looked up as I approached. I climbed down and shoved Lady Renegade's reins in his hand.

"My horse!" I said pointing to Renegade, "Your horse," pointing to Lady Renegade.

He smiled, because he had lost Renegade to the mountain man, and the mountain man had lost the horse to me. Rightfully, Renegade was mine and the gift of Lady Renegade was very generous.

"It is good. You drink, we go."

His english was improving so fast that soon he would be able to hold a conversation. Then maybe he could help me get back to my family.

Chapter Thirteen

Cutting the ragged slivers from the broken end of
the arrow, Jimmy pulled it back through with a quick tug.
Pa cried out in pain, even though he was still unconscious.

"We best get him back to the wagons. He's lost a lot
of blood," Jimmy said, tearing off a piece of Pa's shirt tail
and tying it securely around the wound.

They lifted him to the back of Jimmy's horse and
led him back to the wagon train as Bob walked along
helping him maintain his balance. It wasn't easy to keep
the unconscious rider from falling out of the saddle, as his
weight shifted back and forth with each step of the horse.

"How bad is he hurt?" Ma cried as the men loaded
Pa into the back of the wagon.

"I don't know," Jimmy replied, sorry that he could-
n't give her anymore information. "He passed out shortly
after he came riding in, and we don't know anything about
why they were chasing him, or what he was doing out
there in the first place."

"We thought Jeremy went after Renegade, and John

went looking for him," Ma said, removing the blood soaked bandage as she talked.

"I should have known. If I had just kept an eye on him after giving him that horse..."

"It won't do any good back thinkin' Jimmy," Ma said "besides you can't watch everyone on the wagon train all the time."

Ma cut open the pant leg exposing a nasty wound, as Jimmy went back to the head of the train. The arrowhead, with its ragged edges, had made quite a gash going in and coming out the other side. She cleaned it meticulously with hot water, while she picked out the fibers of cloth the arrowhead had forced into the cut along its path. Ripping some fresh material, she made a new bandage with which she could apply a poultice on each side of the wound. This would draw out any poison or infection, and now all she could do was wait. The hours dragged by as Ma sat watching for any change in Pa's condition.

"It'll be all right Ma," Misty said in her gentle voice, trying to sound more convinced than she really was.

Ma smiled weakly. "I know sweetheart, I'm just a little worried. Your Pa's sleeping now and has no fever, so he'll be all right when he gets his strength back, it's Jeremy I'm worried about."

" Indians!" Pa shouted as he sat bolt upright in bed trying desperately to find his rifle.

"It's ok," Ma said taking hold of his shoulders. "They're gone now. Where is Jeremy?"

Pa looked around the wagon realizing everything must be alright and relaxed a little. "He's with Runs with the Wind. I saw them together on the hill right before the Comanches attacked me."

Ma told him about the Cheyenne chasing off the Comanches before they got to the wagon train, and then riding away without a backward glance.

Breathing a sigh of relief now that the Comanche no

longer posed a threat he sank back into the soft blankets saying, "Good, the boys should be back soon then."

It was no time until he was sleeping soundly. Ma was doing better too, knowing that I was no longer in real danger. Other than Pa, I don't think there was anyone she would have rather had out there with me than Runs with the Wind.

It was late afternoon the next day when Jimmy spotted a man hobbling in from the north. He rode out to find a badly bruised and battered mountain man hopping along with a crooked stick for a crutch.

"Name's Jimmy," he said, pulling his horse to a stop.
"I'm scoutin' for the wagon train back yonder."

"Friends call me T.J." the mountain man said, squinting up at him through two badly swollen black eyes.

His nose was a little crooked, from the clubbing he'd taken, and blood was smeared down the front of his shirt. His deer skin pants were slightly torn below one knee in the back, exposing a nasty bruise and there was a noticeable lump on his head, just above one ear. Even if he knew the man, Jimmy was sure he wouldn't recognize him now.

"Indians?" he asked.

"Yea, they stole my horse, and my plunder."

"Looks like you'll live," Jimmy said, looking over the man who had obviously met more than his match.

"Why shucks, they never put a scratch on me. I got this tryin' to get another horse. I caught a young Cheyenne boy drinkin' from a seep, and clobbered him on the noggin. As I was catchin' the horse, another boy jumped me from behind. Before I knew it there was kickin', bitin', and head clubbin' goin' on like crazy. One of 'em smashed my foot with a rock while the other one busted my nose with a club. Now, I ain't heard of no captives around here, but that second boy was surely white."

"Was one of the horses a bay mare, or a chestnut

gelding with a white blaze on his forehead?" Jimmy asked, already sure of the answer.

"Sure enough. It was that chestnut that the Indian boy was ridin'. You know 'em?"

"How are they now?"

"Last time I saw 'em they was commin' at me like a couple of wildcats. After that I don't know. I was still sleeping face down in the dirt when they left. I didn't have much, but they took my coon skin cap, I still ain't figured that one out yet."

"Here," Jimmy said, reaching out a hand, "climb up. I know some folks that'll want to hear about this."

The wagon train had made it's evening stop when Jimmy and T.J. came riding up to our wagon.

"Is John awake?" Jimmy asked as Ma looked up from the fire where she was cooking.

"I think so. Why?"

"T.J. here has an interesting story for the two of you."

"Misty, see if your Pa's awake."

"Ok Ma," she said running to the back of the wagon.

"Pa, there's a man here to see you. Should I bring him around."

"No, I think I'll come out there, I've been working on this crutch and I think I'll give her a try."

With Misty's help and his new crutch, Pa eased himself out of the wagon and tested his weight on the injured leg. It wasn't as bad as he thought it would be, and he was able to limp around to the front of the wagon.

"Howdy," Pa said, extending his hand to the new comer. As he looked the man over, the wound in his leg didn't seem so bad. This man had obviously been in a real tussle.

T.J. told Pa the story of his encounter with me and Runs with the Wind, and Pa told him how we came to be out there. They talked for quite a while, and Ma asked him to stay and eat.

"Ya know," T.J. said, looking up from his third bowl of stew, "that's quite a lad you got there. To befriend that Indian boy, have him steal his horse, and then fight like that to save his hide. He's gonna be a man to ride the river with. I'd like to meet him, without that club in his hand."

"With the Comanche gone, we thought they would be back by now," Pa said, looking out into the fading light.

"I don't think so. When they left me, they headed north, toward Standing Bear's camp."

"They must think the Comanches are still after them," Ma said, now more worried than before. "How are we going to find him John?"

"I'll help," T.J. stated flatly. "If you can lend me a horse. I know right where they're headed."

"I think I can get you a horse," Pa said, looking across the fire, "but I thought you and the Cheyenne didn't get along."

"Shucks, me and Standing Bear get along just fine. Some of the younger braves steal my horse and supplies two or three times a year. Then I go out and steal some back. It's like a game to them. We've been at it for years, and nobody's got hurt serious yet. Except this last time, I don't think those boys knew it was a game."

"I'll see if I can get you a horse and we'll leave in the morning," Pa said, pulling himself up on his crutch.

"Good enough. There and back shouldn't take more than four days. Wouldn't mind if I had another bowl of that stew, would ya M'am? I wouldn't want to see it go to waste," T.J. said helping himself one more time.

Chapter Fourteen

We left the water hole heading north, with the mountain man still laying in the dirt. His breathing was shallow, but I didn't mention it to Runs with the Wind for fear he might want to finish the job. To my relief he gathered up his bow and arrows and walked away. He started to get on his horse and changed his mind. He walked back over to where the man lay face down in the dirt, and picked up his coon skin cap. Placing it ceremoniously on his head, he looked down at the hapless figure and stated flatly, "Next time you'll know me," in his native language. Then swinging to his horse's back he let out a war cry and headed north at a lope. He was just letting off steam after a heated battle and I have to admit I surprised myself, when I did my best imitation of him. He stopped in his tracks, turning to look at me racing along behind, yelling my head off. It was exhilarating and we both laughed as we rode off together with our backs straight, our heads high, and our horses prancing along. We were quite a sight and feeling pretty good about ourselves.

We were so busy impressing each other that we didn't see the big mamma grizzly bear with the two cubs until we were almost on her. She was only thirty yards away, and when she stood up on her hind legs, she was looking us right in the eyes.

With an earth shattering roar she dropped to all fours making a short charge. Our horses were bucking and kicking at everything in sight. I had never seen one before, but I knew if I didn't stay on that horse, I wouldn't live long enough to see another.

Before I knew what was happening, my horse was running recklessly back down the trail, with Lady Renegade right on his heels. Both of us were hanging on for dear life as the branches of the trees tried to rip us from the horses backs.

I didn't know how far she chased us, but we were almost back to the spring by the time we regained control of our mounts. Runs with the Wind took the lead and went up the steep hillside to the ridge above the water hole. Reaching the top, we could see more open country to the east, and opted to go that way instead. Better to go a little out of the way than to chance meeting that mamma bear again.

We circled wide to the east, into the smoother rolling hills, where the buffalo grass was more abundant than any other plant. At least here we could see what we were getting into, before it was to late.

There was no telling where the wagon train was now. I had no idea how far we had traveled, or which directions we had gone. It seemed like there was always something making us change our path. It was a strange country, everything looked the same, except those magnificent blue mountains with the white caps on top. We could see them to the west from any rise we happened to be on. If I only lived there, it would be easy to get home, you could find that high peak without hardly trying.

Around noon I got a startling surprise. As we climbed over a large rolling hill, we could see a herd of buffalo slowly grazing along in our path. There were thousands of the critters. Cows with calves, yearlings, and huge bulls with massive front shoulders, and big shiny black horns that rang out like gunfire when they ran head long into each other, fighting for supremacy. I was awed by the sight of them stretching out from horizon to horizon and as far ahead as we could see.

Runs with the Wind didn't have to tell me that we couldn't ride through them, I could see that was much too dangerous. We dare not go back to the west, for fear of the she bear coming out onto the plains in search of a sick or wounded member of the herd. So once again we turned to the east making our journey that much longer.

All day we traveled along the fringes of the buffalo herd. Sometimes we thought we were going around the end, and headed north, to find it was only a pocket where we would have to back track south to get around.

That evening we stopped to rest at a small stream, well within earshot of the bellowing of the bulls and bleating of the calves. It seemed like forever since we had eaten, and when a yearling calf walked into the trees along the stream a hundred yards away, Runs with the Wind took his bow and started working quietly from tree to tree. I had hunted with Pa some and fell in behind, staying far enough back not to spoil his shot. He worked along so slow and silent that I thought the calf would be a full grown bull by the time we got there.

After what seemed like hours, he slowly started raising his bow. Swish... He drew the arrow back and shot so fast I didn't even see it. The arrow hit with a light thud and sank to the feathers behind the front shoulder.

The calf let out a startled cry. Busting out of the trees toward the main herd, he fell to the ground with a thump, bawling and kicking up dust. Instantly the nearest of the buffalo were running blindly bumping into others, increasing the panic. It was like a wave across the water picking up momentum as it went. Soon they were all running as far as the eye could see. Great clouds of dust were billowing up everywhere, and the ground was shaking under our feet. The stampede was so loud you couldn't hear yourself think. Then as suddenly as it started they were gone, nothing left but the dust slowly settling in the soft evening breeze, and one yearling calf with Runs with the Wind's arrow buried in his chest.

As we cleaned the animal, Runs with the Wind sliced off pieces of the liver with his hunting knife and began eating them as he worked. He offered me some, and being very hungry, I gave it a try. It was the strangest, nastiest thing I had ever put in my mouth. I couldn't spit it out fast enough.

"Hungry I might be," I told him, "but if you don't mind I like mine cooked."

With a look of contempt on his face, he shrugged his shoulders and went back to the task at hand.

It was a lot of work, taking over an hour to skin the carcass and cut off the choice meat for cooking. I built a small fire and put two large chunks on a spit while he finished cutting the rest of the meat off the bones. We split the hide in two equal pieces and laid the meat out to cool in the evening breeze while we ate.

To this day I have never tasted anything finer than freshly roasted buffalo hump. We ate with our fingers, grease running down to our elbows, until I thought I would bust.

That night, as we sat by the fire, talking and reliving the past few days, I realized I would never be a farmer like Pa. This was the life for me, roaming wild and free. Taking from the land only what I needed to survive, and leaving the rest to enjoy later. Yes, this would be the perfect life someday, but right now I needed to find a way home.

Chapter Fifteen

The following morning we were up before the sun, preparing packs out of the two sections of buffalo hide. We needed them to carry the meat as we traveled. Runs with the Wind was as skilled at his work, as he was fast. In minutes he had both packs ready to load on the horses. It was going to be another warm day, so we needed to get to the village to keep the meat from spoiling. Neither one of us wanted to take the time to rig up drying racks and cure the meat, when it could easily be done later.

Runs with the Wind assured me it wasn't far to his home and that we would be there by lunch. We moved along at a fast walk, sometimes leading our horses to give them a rest from the extra loads they were carrying. They had worked mighty hard over the last few days and the light forage along the way was starting to drain their strength. It didn't matter now, a few more miles and we could all rest.

At the top of one of the roughest hills we had climbed that morning, he pointed to the end of the valley and said, "There."

"Is that your home?" I asked.

"Yes, I live there," he replied kicking his horse back into a walk.

"Runs with the Wind is this going to be ok, me coming along, and all?" I asked starting to think about the possible consequences for the first time.

"It is good. You come."

"I know it's all right with you, what about the rest of your people?"

"I tell them, you brother. Do not worry."

His command of the english language was getting better by the hour, while my use of Cheyenne was very poor at best.

Drawing closer to the village we began to notice something strange. We saw no smoke from the fires, nor could we hear any voices. There should have been dogs barking and the sound of children playing, but there was only silence.

My hopes for a solution fell like a stone when we saw what was left of the abandoned campsite. They had been gone for a couple of days or more by the looks of things, and I started to follow the trail left by the travois.

"Wait," he said, riding up to me.

He pointed to the meat pack on my horse and indicated that we needed to take care of it before it ruined. Reluctantly, I conceded that he was right, and began gathering wood for the fires as he restored several drying racks that had been left behind. We worked the rest of the day, and into the night, drying the meat over fires that were hot enough they cooked it as much as they dried it out.

"Tomorrow we go," he said replacing some of the jerked meat with fresh strips. "We catch fast. They go slow."

The next morning we started following them straight toward the high peak of the shining mountains. The terrain was getting rougher, and the trees were getting thicker. We left the gentle rolling hills behind us and headed into the rougher country along a well established trail. From the looks of it, the Cheyenne had been using it for many generations.

"Where are they going?" I asked.

"Sun Dance, in the land of the mountain tribe."

At least we were headed west. That would put me closer to the wagon train when I got a chance to go back.

We rode along at a ground eating trot, making up time on the rest of his people, who could only travel at a slow steady walk. They couldn't go any faster, or the little children and old ones could not keep up. It didn't matter to them, they allowed plenty of time when they traveled. The young warriors would scout and hunt along the way to relieve their boredom, and the women spent their time gossiping and enjoying the break in the daily work routine.

It was nearly two full days before one of the rear scouts came out of the trees in the trail ahead.

"We thought you were dead," he said in his own language, to Runs with the Wind, refusing to acknowledge my presence.

"I had a little trouble," he replied, "but nothing my friend and I couldn't handle."

I couldn't understand the words, but I was sure there was no love lost between these two.

He was bigger than Runs with the Wind and looked to be stronger too. I couldn't see any reason for him to be jealous, but the look of it was in his eyes.

"Who is he?" I asked as we followed him down the well beaten trail.

"Spotted Horse," he replied, "he wanted me to die."

He tried to explain, but his english wasn't good enough yet. I found out later, that Night Hawk had warned Spotted
Horse's brother, Little Feather, about going on a vision quest earlier in the Spring. Night Hawk had told him that he was not ready and it would be to dangerous. He didn't

listen to the Medicine man and went anyway. Little Feather was killed by a puma, and Spotted Horse thought it would be good revenge if Night Hawks only son were to die on a vision quest also.

We caught up to the travelers when they stopped for the night. Runs with the Wind's father could barely maintain the dignity of his position when he saw the son he thought he had lost. His mother, Quail, didn't try. She ran up hugging him and talking so fast no one could understand her.

"I am well mother," he told her. "I am a warrior not a child to be cried over."

She stepped back and looked at him through different eyes. Eyes that were proud of the son she had raised.

"Welcome back," Night Hawk said trying to hold an even voice.

"Thank you, father. This is my friend Jeremy, I call him Brother of the Wind. He has helped me through my travels and given me this horse as a token of friendship."

"Jeremy," Night Hawk spoke in fluent english, "welcome to our camp. Runs with the Wind considers you his brother and I will welcome you into my lodge as a son."

No wonder Runs with the Wind picked up our language so fast. He probably had a lot of it stored in his memory from hearing his father speak it.

"Runs with the Wind, tell me how is it that you leave here with nothing and return with Comanche weapons, a white mans horse, the hat of a mountain man, and a friend who's language you don't even speak? And you had time to hunt fresh meat along the way. Tell me, why didn't you slay the great bear while you were at it?" Night Hawk could no longer control his laughter.

Runs with the Wind winked at me as he said, "We thought about it."

Chapter Sixteen

"I just want to borrow the horse, Jimmy. You'll get him back in a few days," Pa said, trying to persuade Jimmy that he was right.

"I trust you John, but if you go out there with that crazy old mountain man you may not come back at all."

"If you're worried about not getting your horse back, I'll pay you for him. That way you stand to lose nothing."

"It's not the horse John. What's Cheryl and Misty goin' to do if you don't come back. It's like I keep tellin' ya. This is a hard land with tough choices, you got to learn to make the right ones."

"Fine, I'll get the horse somewhere else."

"No. If you're set on goin', then you can take the horse. Just don't expect much, there's a lot of country out there, and anything can happen."

"Thanks Jimmy, I knew I could count on you."

"Don't thank me yet, I don't believe I'm doin' you any favor."

wagon, where he picked up T.J. amd headed north before
the wagons started rolling. Barring any problems they
would make it to Standing Bear's camp in two days. Pa
was anxious to hurry along, but T.J. convinced him to spare
the horses.

"There's nothing but time out here John, no sense in
hurrying along."

"Jeremy's only fourteen, and probably scared half
to death."

"He's in Standing Bears camp by now. If he's all
right today, he'll be all right tomorrow. Besides, you said
yourself, that him and that Cheyenne boy were as thick as
thieves."

"You're probably right T.J., at least I sure hope you
are."

By noon they had reached the spot where we first
met T.J.   Watering their horses, he showed Pa where the
ruckus had taken place. Following our trail north, it
wasn't long before they came upon our tracks, where we
had raced back down the trail and up the steep slope to the
east.

"I wonder, what made them change their minds?"
Pa asked.

"I don't know. We can take a look see, if you want."
T.J. said, already starting up the trail.

He hadn't gone a hundred yards when he stopped
abruptly. "Grizz," he said looking into the trees all around.
"A she bear with youngens, and she may have a den close
by. Best follow the advice of the boys, and put some distance between us."

There was no argument as they turned their horses
back down the trail. By late afternoon, they encountered
the same large herd of buffalo that we had. This easy trip,
was becoming longer and more complicated all the time,
and Pa's patience was wearing thin as they headed east.

"Don't worry about it John. The boys made the

same detour, we're not losin' any ground."

"We're not making up any either. Isn't there any way to go through them?"

"Not in one piece there ain't. We'll get there."

By noon the next day they were able to swing north, several miles west of where we did, thanks to the stampede caused by the yearling Runs with the Wind had shot.

That evening they reached the deserted Cheyenne camp just before dark. Pa's heart sank when he discovered they had left to move west. He walked through the empty camp with a feeling of helplessness and despair. In frustration he kicked over a drying rack that Runs with the Wind had restored to cure our meat on.

"John, look at this. These three drying racks, and the one you kicked over. Somebody's set these up and used 'em after the Cheyenne left. Them boys, I'm bettin'. They killed themselves a young buffalo and took the time to dry the meat. We're gaining on them now."

"You think so?" Pa said more hopeful now than ever.

"Sure. Tell you what. The moon's coming up bright, and the trail is easy to follow, let's mosey along a while and pick up some more time on 'em," T.J. could sense the need in Pa to stay on the trail. "Shoot, at this rate, we'll catch 'em in no time."

They walked along in the moonlight, both knowing there would be no sleeping on this night, save what they could do in the saddle. Pa finally felt like he was getting close and there was no stopping him now. If T.J. had refused to go on, Pa would have left him behind for sure.

Chapter Seventeen

There would be no lodges set up until they reached the location of the Sun Dance, so we sat around Night Hawk's fire that evening, telling tales of our adventures. Runs with the Wind was an excellent story teller, and had the audience constantly edging closer to hear every detail. Night Hawk translated for me, so I wouldn't be left out. Once in a while he would ask me a question or two, making me think that Runs with the Wind had left something out. Each time I answered, he would smile and nod with a pleased expression on his face. After a while I figured out that he was checking to see if our stories matched.

When he told the part about our encounter with T.J. he had to stop several times to let the laughter die down, to where he could be heard again. As he finished he picked up the coon skin cap from where it lay near his feet, and put it on, causing a cheer to explode from the crowd.

When he had finished many of the young warriors

came forward to ask questions, and praise his valor. All those present were seeing him in a new light. One that he wore quite well. I heard him mention my name, and as one body, they were all staring at me.

"Go on," he told them, "he doesn't bite."

Slowly, and with some encouragement, they came forward. Runs with the Wind would introduce each one, and they would clasp my hand or put a hand on my shoulder smiling as Night Hawk translated for me. All came to greet me, except Spotted Horse, who remained in the shadows at the edge of the firelight. He was not happy about the return of Runs with the Wind, and even less pleased with his reception. This was a deep resentment that went well beyond reason. It overflowed from Night Hawk, to his son, and now to me.

Night Hawk held up his hands and asked for quiet.

"Know this," he spoke in Cheyenne, "all that are here, Runs with the Wind has found his kindred spirit in Jeremy. They have been brothers for all time. For this reason he shall always be welcome in my lodge, and treated as a member of my family."

"You know, they consider you something of a hero," Night Hawk said patting me on the shoulder. "You will be as well protected in our village as any other member of the tribe."

Yet I couldn't help but remember the scowl on Spotted Horse's face. I began to wonder if Night Hawk knew how deep that resentment had grown. One thing was for sure, I wasn't going to turn my back on him as long as I was in the Cheyenne camp.

It was the following morning before I got a chance to speak to Night Hawk about going back to the wagon train.

"Night Hawk," I started, as we walked along the trail.

"You should call me father. As you are now like a son to me, it is expected."

His tone was so matter of fact, and sounded as if he expected me to be there forever, that it took me by surprise.

"Father," I started again, not wanting to anger him, "I must get back to my family, but I could never find them now."

"I have spoken to Standing Bear on this. We feel that you should go to the Sun Dance. As the kindred spirit of Runs with the Wind, he will need your support. After the Sun Dance is over we will take you to your people."

"How long will that be?" I asked not able to believe he was going to make me go whether I wanted to or not.

"By the new moon, or shortly after you will be back with your family."

"That's too long. Pa's probably out looking for me right now. I know Ma's worried sick."

"Is there someone there who speaks Cheyenne?"

"Jimmy can, he's the scout."

"Good. This too, I have spoken to Standing Bear about. We will send a runner to let your family know you are well. They will know that the Sun Dance is very important and must be seen to first."

"I'm not so sure. I've been here a while and I still don't know why it's important."

"The Sun Dance is not just a dance. It's a pledge of ourselves to the spirits. Our way of promising to live our lives the way it was intended. It's a time of personal sacrifice, when each dancer, dances for the entire village. There is great personal pain and self-denial. The dancers must go without food or drink through four days and nights of preparation. They will sit in a medicine lodge filled with smoke from the cedar boughs purifying themselves for the dance on the evening of the fourth day. At that time we will use a bone awl to pierce the skin and muscle on each side of the chest so a wooden skewer may be pushed through. The skewers will be attached, by ropes, to a pole in the center of the camp. The dancers will pray to the spirits and blow on whistles made of eagle bone, while they throw themselves backward trying to pull free. It lets the spirits know how serious their prayers are, and helps to make the visions clear. That's how the ones who have gone before let us know what needs to be done in our lives. This is why Runs with the Wind will need your help. You're his kindred spirit. Your strength will be his strength, his pain will be shared by you, making him stronger. He is a brave young man, but in this, he must have your help."

"I think I understand," I said, noting his serious approval. "Tell me more about the spirits."

We talked for most of the day as we traveled. Runs with the Wind was busy with his friends, and I felt comfortable in the company of his father. He told me his beliefs and I told him mine. There were many things I could learn from him, if I just didn't need to find a way back home.

Chapter Eighteen

The wagon train had reached the lower foot hills of the shining mountains by the time Gray Wolf caught up to them. It had been a pleasant ride so far. It was nice to have a change of scenery, after spending so much time on the plains. Here the oaks grew thick with intermittent pines. Scattered through the mountains were large patches of aspen, where fires had burned out the old growth. There were few buffalo here, but the deer and elk were abundant. There were marmots and badgers, coyotes and cougars, and many other small animals and birds. There was always something to look at, but one must always be vigilant. You never knew when you might happen upon an enemy. You had to learn to enjoy nature with one eye, and watch for danger with the other.

Finding the wagon train was the easy part. Now he had to find the one man on it that he could talk to, without getting shot by some trigger happy traveler that was afraid of his own shadow. Grey Wolf had known men before, who professed bravery, yet shied away from conflict at any cost. He would deliver the message one way or another. Standing Bear had entrusted him with this task, and thought it very important. He would not fail. He would not allow himself to fail.

Even as these thoughts went through his mind, the giant bear came out of the thick oak brush only three or four paces in front of him. The grizzly came fast, rising to his hind legs, and slapping his horse with a huge paw. Gray Wolf's mount fell instantly with a broken neck, sending him rolling through the brush. Still standing to his full height of ten feet, the bear roared, pawing at the air as he came forward. Gray Wolf scrambled for his bow lying only a few feet away. The string had been broken in the fall, as were most of his arrows. There was no way to out run a bear, and he didn't have a decent weapon to fight with. If only he had a spear, then he would have a chance. In desperation he grabbed an arrow with his right hand and his knife with his left. This was going to be close fighting, to the death, with no way out.

"Keep standing tall," Gray Wolf said to the bear as it continued to come at him. "Two more steps. You may kill me, but you'll regret the day you found Gray Wolf."

The bear kept coming. One step, two steps, Gray Wolf ducked under a sweeping paw that was primed to take his head off. He threw himself against the bear, driving the arrow upward through his heart. The giant bear came down on him, biting and slashing with six inch claws. His teeth came together smashing bone and nearly taking off the left leg above the knee. Only death stopped the bear from tearing Gray Wolf apart.

He was hurt bad and needed help. The only hope he had, was to reach the people to whom he was supposed to deliver the message.

Gray Wolf cut away the leg of his deer skin pants to get to the nasty wound. Somehow the bear had not managed to tear the main artery in his leg, even though the damage was extensive. He cut the deer skin in thin strips and began making a bandage.   Needing more leather, he cut the other pants leg off above the knee and pulled it over the torn flesh. Tying the thin strips above and below the ripped and exposed muscles, he effectively slowed the bleeding. It also served to keep out the dirt.

By the time the bandage was complete, he could hear the first wagons coming up the steep slope only a long bow shot away.   He tried to stand, but there was no strength in his good leg and it gave out almost immediately. Falling to the ground he started crawling toward the sound of the wagons. One by one, he heard them pass as he clawed desperately at the brush. His progress was slow at best, and the pain was so intense, his vision blurred. In the fading light of dusk, a small part of him wanted only to sleep.

Fighting off the distractions he continued on his way. Much closer now, he could hear voices but, his eyes refused to work. He tried to yell, managing only a hoarse plea for help. The will to continue was strong, though his body would not cooperate. But he must go on. He had given his word to Standing Bear.

"Ma, look!" Misty cried, pointing to the brush beside the trail.

"I don't see anything," she replied, continuing on her way.

"It was a man, and he's hurt bad," Misty said straining to see back around the wagon.

"Are you sure?" Ma asked pulling the wagon to a stop.

"What's wrong up there?" Mr. Roberts yelled, wondering why they had come to a stop.

"Misty says she saw a man in the brush back there. She said he was hurt bad."

Searching the foliage, Mr. Roberts caught sight of the brightly colored bead work on Gray Wolf's buckskin shirt. He jumped from his wagon seat and went for a closer look. Gray Wolf was unconscious by the time he got there, but still alive.

"It's an Indian," he said "He's alive, but just barely."

"Misty, run ahead and fetch Jimmy, I'm going to see if I can help."

Ma, Mr. Roberts and Mrs. Roberts carried Gray Wolf to the back of our wagon and laid him inside. It seemed like there was always something, or someone riding in that spot, that needed help. By the time Jimmy got there Ma and Mr. Roberts had dressed the wound, and tied a splint around the leg, holding the broken bone in place.

"He's Cheyenne," Jimmy said, fingering the bead work on Gray Wolf's shirt. "What do you plan to do with him?"

"Take care of him, I guess," Ma said, never thinking otherwise.

"What if he ain't friendly?" Jimmy's tone was getting harsh.

"How unfriendly could he be in that condition?"

"I don't know," Jimmy told her. "You just call me as soon as he's awake."

"Don't worry," Mr. Roberts said, "I'll ride back here with my rifle on him till we know."

Jimmy left muttering something about people needing to learn to mind their own business. Gray Wolf didn't wake up until the next morning while Ma was cooking breakfast. Pa always said, the smell of her biscuits and coffee would wake up anybody. Misty heard him groan, and peeked in the back to see if he was awake. She was greeted by a gentle smile and the words "Hello, Little Sun Spirit," in Cheyenne.

"Ma, he knows me!"

"How could he know you child? We've never seen him before."

"He called me Little Sun Spirit in Cheyenne, just like Runs with the Wind used to."

"Are you sure?" Without waiting for an answer she

said, "Go get Jimmy, and hurry."

Jimmy translated the message to Ma and Misty, causing a sigh of overwhelming relief. Ma was so grateful about the news he brought that she hugged him and gave him a kiss on the cheek.

"Gray Wolf says, for that, he would have fought two bears," Jimmy said, laughing under his breath.

For the first time in many days Ma laughed out loud.

"What about John?" She asked.

"He hadn't seen him. But most likely he's caught up with them by now. I'm sure he's all right."

"You tell Gray Wolf to just rest easy. We'll take care of him until his people come.

Since they had stopped for the night shortly after finding Gray wolf, Jimmy followed his trail back through the brush. He had gone little more than a hundred yards, when he came upon the bear. It was laying on its side leaving the fatal wounds plainly visible. There were several stab wounds made by Gray Wolf's knife, but the one that did the trick, was the arrow through the heart. Jimmy picked up the bow with the broken string, and looked again to the bear. The string had been broken before the arrow was placed. Gray Wolf had used the arrow as a small spear.

He removed the bears claws, tucking them in his pocket. Picking up the bow and arrows, he headed back to the wagons. He told Ma the story as he gave Gray Wolf what was left of his weapons. The bear claws, he left in his pocket, to be laced on to a leather thong that night. A necklace of claws that large would be considered strong medicine among the Cheyenne, and would bring Gray Wolf much prestige. It would be good medicine for him too, while he recovered from the fight.

That night, when Jimmy brought the bear claw necklace to the wagon and hung it around Gray Wolf's neck, a bond was formed that could never be broken.

Chapter Nineteen

As we looked into the valley where the Sun Dance was to be held, runners told the camp of our coming. Many villagers came out to greet the new arrivals. Some were relatives and others were old friends anxious to hear any new gossip.

It was a breathtaking view, with a large waterfall cascading down the rock cliffs in the background. A large stream ran around the edge of the campsite, providing enough clean water for all. There had been a light rain the night before, and the crisp morning air was filled with the scent of pine, cedar, and aspen. The hill to the east was covered with grass and bright yellow wild flowers. To the west was the ever present peak of the Shining Mountains. From where I stood I could see the snow covered rocks above the tree line. It was hard to imagine a place so high that nothing would grow there but a few tiny plants.

The village itself, seemed to be separated into groups, forming a circle. We were the last to arrive, and already vividly ornamented tepees nearly covered the valley.

The chief from the northern Cheyenne came to

show us where to set up the lodges. It was their turn to host the Sun Dance and he made a great show of the responsibility. He greeted Standing Bear, and of course Night Hawk, as was customary. When his eyes reached me his smile faded and I felt a knot of fear in my stomach.

Night Hawk and Standing Bear told him I was a kindred spirit to Runs with the Wind, who would be participating in the Sun Dance. He didn't seem to be convinced, but being a gracious host, decided to overlook the matter for now. There was no time to waste, lodges needed to be set up and preparations made. The purification of the dancers was ready to begin in the morning.

I did what I could to help erect the lodge of Night Hawk and Quail. I think I did more harm than good, though the effort was appreciated. Their skilled hands deftly tied the knots and lashings. When the skin cover had been raised and the door flap put in place it was a sight to behold. There were paintings, dyed into the hide, depicting both the sun and the moon. On one side was a picture of a buffalo, grazing peacefully in the tall prairie grass. On the other side a large Hawk with talons outstretched, as it swooped down on some unseen prey.

After it was finished I stood back and admired it with pride, as though it were my own.

That night, around the central campfire the story tellers of each tribe, usually the medicine man, told of the events that had taken place in their village during the previous year. This was especially helpful to the other villages in cases of conflict with other tribes or to evaluate the size and locations of the herds. They told of births and of deaths. They told of hard times and prosperity. But mostly they told of things that would bring prestige to their villages.

Night Hawk got up to speak. He walked solemnly to his post of honor, in front of the fire, facing the semicircle of onlookers. The crowd fell silent as he began to speak of the tragic death of Little Feather, which he had been unable to prevent. He told of the new births of two strong boys, and the short lived battle with the Comanche.

Then he began the talk of Runs with the Wind. I knew the story by heart now, and my mind drifted off to the coming Sun Dance.

His mention of my name jolted me back to reality. With my limited use of Cheyenne, I could only catch bits and pieces of what he was saying.

"Jeremy, with hair like the sun, and eyes like the sky, is the spirit brother of Runs with the Wind. They have shared food and drink, and have passed from boys to manhood together. They have done battle with their enemies, both red and white, side by side. They have traveled many days journey across the rolling hills as brothers. This night, I announce to all, that Jeremy is my adopted son. He may come and go as any warrior would, and he will always be welcome in the lodge of Night Hawk.

"Jeremy, come stand with me so all will know who you are."

With a little persuading from Runs with the Wind and Quail, I walked hesitantly to the side of the man I now referred to as father.

"Runs with the Wind, come up here also."

He was not so reluctant to stand in front of a crowd, that had just heard stories of his bravery.

"I show you tonight," Night Hawk began, "two young men, from two separate worlds. They are as different as night and day, yet their spirits found each other in a time of need, so that one might lend it's strength to the other as any brother would. One is dark, and one is light. One speaks the white mans words, and the other, the language of the people, yet their spirits are woven together like a fine rope."

To me he said, "Give me your hand."

As I held it out, he produced a razor sharp knife.

"Don't show any pain," he whispered, and then

made a shallow cut across my palm. I stood there with my hand out, dripping blood, as he repeated the process on Runs with the Wind. He then held our hands high in the air so everyone could see. Pushing our bleeding palms together he proclaimed, "Their spirits have been brothers from the beginning of time, now they are brothers in blood also. From this day forward, Jeremy is Cheyenne, and shall be known throughout our land as Brother of the Wind."

Shouts of approval rose from the crowd. Mostly, I think, from our own village.

"My son," it was Quail, but she wasn't talking to Runs with the Wind, she was speaking to me. "You will need these for the Sun Dance," she said shoving a bundle into my hands. It was the first time I had ever heard her speak english. "Go ahead, open it."

It was a new set of buckskins. Complete with brightly colored beadwork, and fringe down the arms and legs, as well as a new pair of moccasins. Hours of hard work had gone into making these knew clothes, and I really meant it when I said, "Thank you mother."

Chapter Twenty

We were already in the medicine lodge cleansing our bodies and new buckskins in the purifying smoke of the green cedar branches, when my Pa reached the village.

"How can we possibly find him down there?" John was looking across the valley that seemed to be overflowing with tepees.

"See that warrior coming up through the trees? He's a lookout.   Providin' he don't come out flingin' arrows, we'll get him to take us to see Standing Bear.   If Jeremy's here, he'll know where."

"We came to see Standing Bear." T.J. called out in Cheyenne.

"Come then," he replied, "I will take you to him."

The warrior was not worried about the two who followed. What could they possibly do against the entire Cheyenne nation. He was sure there would be no trouble, besides he knew T.J. Not to talk to, but he had stolen his horse a time or two in the past. From the looks of him, Night Hawk had been very accurate in his description of the fight between his sons and the mountain man.

They found Standing Bear in the center of the village talking to the other chiefs. He was a man of formality and welcomed the visitors into his camp. When T.J. explained that Pa was my father, he became eager to show his hospitality. My presence had brought a lot of attention to his village. Everyone was talking about Night Hawks new son.

"We came to take Jeremy home," T.J. said.

Standing Bear's mood changed immediately. He was solemn, suddenly not sure he was happy to see the new comers. Jeremy could not leave now, he had started the purification for the Sun Dance. If he left now, it might anger the spirits, and that could be disastrous. He would not allow it. After the Sun Dance, when the tribes split up, then Brother of the Wind could go back. If, he chose to.

"Come," Standing Bear said, "we will speak with Night Hawk on this matter."

As they walked through the village, following the chief who was dressed in his finest attire, T.J. whispered to Pa, "John, something is goin' on here we don't know about. No matter what happens don't lose you temper. They have a high regard for honor, as long as we behave like guests we'll be treated well. If we step out of line, we won't see the sun set."

At Night Hawks lodge they were greeted like family. Pa was glad to find that Night Hawk spoke english. Finally he could speak for himself, without someone else putting their own meaning to his words.

"I have come for Jeremy," he said, "I'm told he is with you."

"He stays in my Lodge," Night Hawk replied trying to think of a way to tell this man that he had just adopted his son. He knew the white mans words but not his customs on such matters.

"I have been traveling for several days, and I would like to get back to the wagon train as soon as possible."

"When the Sun Dance is over you may take him and leave, as I said in my message to you. But he must stay until it is completed."

"What message? I've talked to no one until now."

"When Jeremy first arrived here we sent a runner to the wagon train so you would not worry. He was to tell you that we would bring your son back to you after the ceremony."

"Thank you, but I'm here now, so I'll take him back."

"It is good. In four days the Sun Dance will be over, and you may go."

"I prefer to go now," John was beginning to lose his temper.

"You may go, Jeremy stays!"

"Why?" John was furious now, "is he a prisoner?"

"No, he is not a prisoner, he is my son also. Come into my lodge. There is much to explain. It would be better for us to talk of this alone."

As Night Hawk spoke to the chief, Pa told T.J. to wait outside. He was going to get to the bottom of this somehow.

He followed as Night Hawk led the way into the lodge. They circled the small fire in the middle, sitting in the back to face the door. Quail offered him some jerked buffalo and a gourd cup filled with a cool liquid. It seemed to be some kind of tea made of herbs. It was sweet and refreshing, helping him to relax somewhat, under the stressful circumstances.

"To begin with," Night Hawk started , "many things have happened since our sons were brought together. Their spirits have been brothers since the beginning of time, and now they must stand together to face an important ordeal."

"What kind of ordeal? Is Jeremy in some kind of danger?"

"No, this is an ordeal of the spirits. They are linked,

and draw strength from one another. Did T.J. not tell you of their encounter?"

"Yes he told me. How do you know him?"

"I have stolen a horse or two from him myself."

Both men laughed, easing the tension a little further, and Night Hawk continued.

"Since they are brothers in spirit, I adopted Jeremy as a son, and he has decided to help Runs with the Wind through the Sun Dance. My son is strong, but he is very young to dance in this ceremony. Jeremy will purge himself and then sit on the grass near the dancers, praying to the spirits, while his own spirit lends its strength to Runs with the Wind. It is the most important ceremony of the season and it has already begun. To interfere with them now could bring disaster to us all. No one in the village would let you take him away now. Be patient on this. I tell you these things as a friend and because our sons share the same spirit. T.J. can go tell the others that you are well and will be returning soon. Until then you will stay in my lodge as an honored guest."

They talked for a long time and Pa could see no way out other than to stay, so he sent T.J. back with the message.

"Take the horse back to Jimmy for me, and I'll see what I can do about getting you one of your own when I get back. Tell Cheryl not to be concerned, and that we'll catch up in a few days."

"T.J.," Night Hawk spoke solemnly, "accept this gift from me, and my new friend."

Quail stepped around the lodge leading a big pinto.

"That's my horse," T.J. blurted.

"Yes, I know he was your horse once. Now he is yours again."

Even T.J. laughed as he took the reins figuring Night Hawk would probably have him back before to long.

Chapter Twenty One

"Night Hawk," Pa said as T.J. rode away, "what am I supposed to do while this ceremony is taking place?"

"Do what you wish. You are a guest, to come and go as you please."

"I can leave if I want?"

"As long as Jeremy is not disturbed."

Night Hawk could see that Pa was feeling out of place, and began working on a plan to make him more comfortable with the situation.

"Maybe you would like to hunt or scout a little. After many days of traveling to reach the Sun Dance it would be good to have fresh meat. It would be better if Quail's brother Antelope went with you, he is well known among the Cheyenne."

"I have no use for the meat, and I am only concerned with Jeremy's welfare."

"Your son will be well taken care of while he is here. No one would dare to harm the adopted son of a medicine man."

"If I did go hunting, I wouldn't have a way to take care of the meat, unless you would accept it as a gift for your hospitality to my son."

"Elk meat is always welcome in the lodge of Night Hawk," he said, recognizing Pa for the diplomat he was.

Night Hawk had made it more of a challenge than a suggestion. Pa knew it was to take his mind off of the things he couldn't change, and nothing less than fresh elk meat would be acceptable.

"Why not, I can spend the time hunting instead of sitting here waiting. Tell Antelope I'll be ready in the morning. That arrow I took in the leg is beginning to throb something awful, and right now I need some rest."

"Let me see what I can do for that wound."

As Night Hawk checked his leg, Quail brought a bag of herbs to him. Applying a mixture of grease and plant material, he shook his feathered rattle over the wound and chanted a short prayer.

"Sleep now. You'll feel better in the morning."

Pa drifted off to a heavy sleep, not sure if it was from the exhaustion of the trip or from something in the tea he'd been given. Either way it was a rest that was long over due and he awoke almost totally refreshed the next morning. The pain in his leg was not bad, and he felt like moving around. Today would be a good day to go hunting.

Antelope led the way south through the foot hills of the Shining Mountains. There would be no game close by, due to the large gathering of Cheyenne. Most of the large game animals had moved out of the area soon after the arrival of the first camp. The few that remained were now jerky, or had already been roasted.

To the east, were the endless rolling plains. The first of the migrating buffalo could be seen slowly edging forward through the grass. The main herd was still well behind them. They didn't talk as they rode because Antelope couldn't speak english. He had no use for it. The few white men he had known, had wanted only to trade trinkets for his furs. Either they were fools, or thought him to be one. These were not the kind of men he considered worthy of friendship, and if all white men were like that, why learn their language.

As they rode through the morning Antelope pointed out one game animal after another, to see if Pa was there just to kill something or seriously hunting. Each time Pa would look at the animal and politely shake his head, saying the word elk. That had been the challenge and that's what he would get. Finally Antelope was convinced and stopped pointing out the smaller game to seriously search for the elusive elk.

They changed directions heading for higher ground. It was just after noon, and this would be the hardest part of the day to find them. In the early morning or late evening they would be grazing in open meadows. At the hottest part of the day however, they would be bedded down in the shade, probably on the south slope of a small canyon. Here they could see any danger coming from below, or make a quick escape down hill, from any danger above. There would be a gentle breeze going up the canyon as the warmer air rose from the valleys below. This would make it more comfortable for the elk, while it allowed them to catch the scent of anything coming along the canyon walls.

As Antelope led the way, they rode up a long ridge, staying on the north side. Coming to a place where the ridge leveled out for a ways, they crossed over the top to a small canyon covered with pine and aspen. In the bottom a stream could be plainly heard, as it made its way down through the rocks.

Antelope slowed his pace. His horse would take two or three steps, then stop while the rider scanned the terrain. If the elk were to hear their approach, the tentative steps would sound no different than those of other elk, cautiously working their way along.

Antelope must have gotten his name for his eye sight, because when he first pointed out the young bull with horns growing in velvet, Pa had a hard time finding it.

It was about three hundred yards down the far side of the canyon. He was laying at the base of a sheer cliff with scattered pines to the sides and below.

So far they had not been seen, so they need only to cross the canyon here where it was small, and circle around to the cliff from above. Slowly, they made their way, leaving the horses tied to a tree, some fifty yards short of the bluff.

Pa had eased a shell into the chamber as he started to leave his horse. There was no noise as they inched forward through the scattered pine trees to the rocky ledge. Easing into position they could see several animals, all totally unaware of their presence.

He surveyed the scene carefully, picking out two mature bulls, laying close together. Antelope had been gracious, if not friendly, the whole day and deserved to get something for his troubles.

Pa squeezed the trigger, quickly levering the action to fire at the second bull. It had started to lunge off of the ground causing the bullet to strike to far back. A third shot stopped him before he could run.

Antelope stared at Pa with his mouth agape. He had never seen a long gun that could be shot more than one time without reloading. This was powerful medicine, and news that would be worth repeating to Night Hawk and Standing Bear.

Leading their horses around the rock cliff, they worked their way down to the sight of the kill. Pa started on the biggest bull and pointed to the other, "He's yours," Pa said, making an eating motion and pointing to Antelope, and then the elk.

Antelope nodded as he quickly set to the task. He had his animal skinned and the meat cut from the bones long before Pa. He cut four aspen poles and together they made a travois to carry the meat back to camp. They could side hill for a ways until they reached the top of the canyon, and follow the long ridge down to the flatter ground a couple miles away. From there the going would be much easier, and they would reach camp before sunset.

They arrived at dusk, as Night Hawk came out of the medicine lodge. He spoke to his wife's brother, turning to say, "Antelope says he is grateful that you would share your kill with him," as Quail and Sun Bird, Antelope's wife, began taking care of the meat.

"It was his kill as much as mine. He earned it."

"Friend," Antelope said in Cheyenne, clasping Pa's hand. There was a different look in his eyes now, a look of something seen in a new light.

During the next two days, Pa stayed close to the camp. He had lost me once and wasn't leaving again without me. He was surprised the next morning when Antelope showed up to go hunting again, and seemed to be disappointed when Pa declined. Whenever he went anywhere in the village with Night Hawk or Quail, Antelope was close at hand trying eagerly to understand the strange words.

Pa was beginning to like these people. They were totally honest, and openly friendly to those they trusted. He was sure that anyone who said, Indians weren't civilized, had never spent any time in a Cheyenne village.

Chapter Twenty Two

We spent four days and three nights preparing for the Sun Dance. Night Hawk would come frequently into the small medicine lodge, where the dancers from our village were. He would do small ceremonies with herbs and smoke, or instructing us on procedure. It was on his first such visit that he told me of my fathers arrival, and his willingness to stay.

"Now, Brother of the Wind you may concentrate on the ceremony."

"Yes father," I said remembering that it was expected of me. "But if I am not to dance with the others, what will my part in the ceremony be?"

"That is for the spirits to decide. I can only tell you that it is important for you, and the village, that you be a part of it."

There were five of us in the lodge. Me and four dancers, including Spotted Horse. He would glare at the two of us from time to time, but nothing more. Runs with the Wind noticed it to, and told me to keep my thoughts pure. The spirits would not look favorably on any one with a bad heart. So I avoided his stares to let my concentration work on the task at hand.

I learned the prayers to the rising sun, and for the coming of darkness. Prayers to the spirits that kept the fires in the night sky, to the spirits of the winds, and the spirits that bring the rain. There were prayers for the return of the buffalo, and prayers for the visions.

Most of the dancers seemed to be getting bored after the first day. I had so much to learn, and Runs with the Wind had so much to teach me, that the days seemed to slip away.

The first two days were the hardest. I had never gone a whole day with out eating something, and this fast would last four days. There would also be only a small amount of water to drink during this time. When we emerged on the fourth day, we were expected to be completely purged of earthly things, including personal thoughts. Our bodies and minds needed to be clean to communicate with the spirits.

By the second night, my stomach was in knots and my throat was parched. I wanted to leave the medicine lodge. Nothing could be worth what I was putting myself through. As I started to stand up, Night Hawk was beside me with a hand on my shoulder.

"Be patient my son, this will pass. When it is finished you will understand."

His words had a calming effect on me that cannot be described. The pains in my throat and stomach seemed to subside. Again I started the chant, feeling somewhat refreshed by his presence.

That night, while I slept, my dreams were different than any others I had ever had. They were restless dreams, jumping from one thing to another. Always before my dreams had made some sense, but these made none.

I woke up the third morning, wondering how much more of this I could take. Though the pain in my stomach was gone, my throat was dry and my lips were beginning to crack, but it didn't seem to matter. I had more important things to consider. The sun was already coming up, and I hadn't done my morning prayers. The day passed quickly, with my thoughts running two steps ahead of me, never allowing me to catch up. I didn't realize it was late, until it was already dark, and I was singing praises to the spirits of the night. I don't remember going to sleep that night, though I dreamed of chasing something that was always just out of reach.

When I awoke, I saw the world had changed. The sounds were sharp and crisp. Everything looked shiny and new with vivid colors that jumped out at me.

My prayers to the morning sun had new meaning. It was a glorious day and I was a part of it. I could touch the mountain tops and feel the cool breeze on my face. I could touch the sun, and feel its warmth breathing life into my very soul. It was a feeling of immortality. I don't know how I knew, but I was sure, Runs with the Wind could feel it too.

As Night Hawk led us out of the lodge, the intensity of the day was overwhelming. Everyone in the world seemed to be gathered together for the ceremony. Some I could see, others I could only feel their presence.

Night Hawk instructed me to sit at the edge of the circle while he prepared the dancers. The grass there was lush and green, like a soft pad. I looked up to see my father smiling down at me. Somehow I had never noticed how big he was, or how gentle he could be when he laid a hand on my shoulder. I remember thinking how lucky I was to have two fathers on this day, when everyone else had only one.

The Sun Dance was starting, and Runs with the Wind was the first in line. Night Hawk gave him the whistle made of eagle bone. He placed it between his lips and clenched his teeth on it, as his father pierced the skin on the right side of his chest making a slit through the muscle.

I groaned loudly, not expecting the pain I felt. It was as though I had been stabbed in the chest with a hot poker. Again the pain came, as Night Hawk pierced the other side, and I nearly fell over. I opened my eyes to see everyone looking at me. My father started to reach down, but Quail stopped him.

"It will be all right," she said, tugging at his sleeve. "He is one with Runs with the Wind, and I would not risk two sons, if it were dangerous."

Runs with the Wind blew on the whistle leaning against the ropes. His vision was coming now, assisted by the pain. He saw a brown stallion running through the tall prairie grass. I too, saw a running stallion, only it was white. I could feel the wind in my face, as I ran through the grass under a cloudless sky. I could feel my muscles surging as the ground was devoured by my churning feet. Suddenly I realized that I was the white horse, and Runs with the Wind was the brown one. We were running toward each other across endless fields of time. Turning at the last minute to run side by side, following a great eagle across the plains and through the mountains. Sometimes running together, sometimes alone. Sometimes we would come together, combining our size and strength to run as one great horse across the plains.

After what seemed like hours the eagle circled, heading back toward the place where the vision had started. Now we were running at the head of a large herd. Some of the horses were white, some were brown, while others were a mixture of both.

It was a feeling of freedom and exhilaration I had never known, but Runs with the Wind broke free landing hard on the ground, and the vision was suddenly gone. Night Hawk was there instantly, helping his son to the edge of the circle, where Quail assisted him back to their lodge. With a word from Night Hawk, my father half carried me, following Quail.

A buzz went through the onlookers, as they witnessed the two of us sharing the same vision. There was no denying we were linked in spirit. Night Hawk had been right about us, and his prestige grew among all the Cheyenne.

We had eaten a little, and drank some tea made of herbs after the dance, and I slept soundly that night. It was the peaceful sleep of satisfaction and well being, allowing me to wake up feeling good, and very, very, hungry.

Chapter Twenty Three

With the buffalo close at hand, Standing Bear decided to stay in this camp for a while to hunt and cure the meat. The other villages were already coming down, preparing for the move to their summer camps.

Night Hawk spoke to the spirits on behalf of the hunters, insuring a successful hunt. How could it be otherwise, with such a large herd moving northward only a half days ride to the east. With his part done, he and Runs with the Wind would be free to ride with us back to the wagon train. There was no need for them to hunt, already having enough meat from the young buffalo and the elk that Pa had killed.

Quail had packed us enough food for twice the journey, knowing that Runs with the Wind and I would be eating almost constantly as we traveled. Even when my stomach was full, I felt the need to eat.

We headed south through the foothills, edging ever westward, to intercept the wagons. I had never been in this part of the country, and could not believe the breathtaking scenery. The beautiful valley, where the Sun Dance had taken place, was only the edge of the magnificent Shining Mountains. I'm not sure if it was the after effects of the ceremony, or the normal effects of the mountains, but I felt a part of them. My spirit flew through the shimmering leaves of the aspen, and darted through the pines. I drank freely of the cool mountain streams, and rejoiced in the warmth of the summer sun. I felt that I was part of the natural scheme of nature.

We stopped for the night at the head of a long valley. Large open meadows lined both sides, coming together in the center, separated only by a slow moving stream. The meadows ended on both sides where the fast growing aspen were working their way toward the stream. Above the aspen, pine trees, and then spruce, covering the mountains all the way up to treeline. We could see some of the open ground there, covered with grass and small plants, reaching up to a point where there were only rocks covered with a thin layer of snow. This was the peak I had been watching for many days.

"Where are we headed Pa? I mean after we get back to the wagon train."

"West," he said looking at me strangely.

"We are west," I protested, "How could we ever find a better place than this?"

"This is the Cheyenne's land Jeremy. They may not welcome white settlers."

"Brother of the Wind is Cheyenne," Night Hawk said, liking the idea of having his adopted son close by. "If he wishes to stay here with his family, they would be welcome. The game here is plentiful, and some of the plants are also good to eat."

"I'm a farmer," John said, "I could grow more food in those meadows than we could possibly eat."

"The Cheyenne would gladly trade meat and furs for the extra food you grow," Runs with the Wind was helping me plead my case.

"Well, that would give us a cash crop, to buy necessities at the nearest trading post. Let me think about it, and I'll talk to your mother when we get back."

We all knew he was sold on the idea. Pa never liked living close to to many folks, and everything we needed was close at hand. Pa and Night Hawk set up camp, as Runs with the Wind and I rode around the valley scouting.

As we headed south through the valley the next morning, Pa had an easy feeling about things. He was content, having found such a spot as this to end their long journey. Night Hawk had assured him that the Roberts family would be welcome too, if they stayed close and treated the Cheyenne fairly. Now all he had to do was convince Cheryl and Bob, of what he and Jeremy already knew.

It was late afternoon when we caught up to the wagons. Ma didn't hardly recognize me in my new buckskins. She didn't know whether to beat me, or just hug me to death.

Gray Wolf hobbled slowly around the wagon, using the homemade crutch that Pa had put together, greeting his medicine man, with a large grin on his face.

"Greetings Night Hawk. It took you long enough to find me."

"We thought you had been killed," Night Hawk said, noticing the bad leg and the bear claw necklace he was wearing. "I almost was," Gray wolf replied, "but I have had two beautiful women waiting on me hand and foot, and one must not rush the healing process."

"Aiee!" Night Hawk exclaimed as Misty came out of the trees with an arm load of wood, "you must be the Little Sun Spirit I've heard so much about."

"Are you his father?" she asked pointing to Runs with the Wind.

"Yes, I am Night Hawk."

"I wondered how you knew he called me Sun Spirit."

"The entire Cheyenne village knows of the kindness and gentle ways, of the Little Sun Spirit."

"Yep," I said, "he told 'em all. I think he's sweet on you."

Misty blushed, and busied herself, helping Ma with the cooking. Gray Wolf told Night Hawk and Runs with the Wind about his near fatal encounter with the bear, while Pa began to outline his plan to Ma and Mr. Roberts.

They talked long into the night discussing the possibilities. Some were good, others were not, but in this land you had to take chances to gain anything worthwhile.

It was decided that come morning we would follow Night Hawk and Runs with the Wind, back to the valley. Gray Wolf could ride in the back of the wagon until we got there, giving him a couple more days to recover.

Jimmy had heard talk going up and down the wagon train and came to see for himself. After meeting Night Hawk and hearing Pa's plan, Jimmy looked him square in the face, and said, "John, it's like I keep tellin' ya. This is a hard land, with tough decisions. You keep making the right ones, and you'll do just fine."

Chapter Twenty Four

Pa and Mr. Roberts picked out cabin sights on each side of the creek. That way the houses would be far enough apart to allow for some privacy, yet close enough in times of need. The four of us started chopping down trees and shaping the logs while the women started planting gardens, for our winter supply of food. Will tried to help with the logs, but was to small to be of much help.

The work was hard, and lasted most of the summer. Occasionally we would take off a day or two to hunt fresh meat. We always traveled a half days ride before hunting, so as not to scare the game out of the valley. We wanted them close by when the snows came and we couldn't go far.

The rain came often enough to the valley, the crops nearly took care of themselves, and we had harvested most of the vegetables when the first frost came. Over night the leaves on the aspens started turning from green to gold or bright yellow, while those in the oak thickets turned bright red. The weather had no effect on the pine trees, leaving them a brilliant green. Within a couple weeks the color contrast between the different types of trees, that seemed to grow in clusters, resembled a patchwork quilt.

As the first flakes of snow settled gently into the valley the work was complete. We had cut and stacked a large pile of the wild grass to feed the horses, and had enough wood stacked to last well into the spring.

It was on this day that Runs with the Wind came to our cabin.

"My brother, you have been very busy," he said in almost perfect English.

"My brother has been very busy also, learning English," I replied, impressed with how well he spoke, "Can you stay a few days?"

"My village has moved to a winter camp, one days ride away," he said pointing to the southeast. "I came to see if you would come spend the winter with us. Our father would like to teach you more about the spirits."

"I'd like to, but I don't know how Pa is going to feel about it."

"Have you never gone to visit relatives before?" he asked.

"Now there's an argument my folks will have trouble getting around. Let's go up to the house."

"Look what I found," I said stepping through the front door of the cabin.

Ma turned hesitantly from her cooking, expecting to see a snake or lizard, or some other small critter, the likes of which I had been dragging in all summer.

"Runs with the Wind," she exclaimed, hurrying across the cabin to wrap her arms around him.

She hugged him once, stepping back for another look. Smiling she stepped forward to hug him again.

"Mother please," he said raising a hand to stop her. "I'm a warrior not a child," and he was smiling as he remembered using the same argument on his own mother.

"If you're going to come around here, you better get

used to it," I said slapping him on the back. "It's one of her customs, like your Sun Dance, only it happens all the time."

He stayed with us a couple days looking over the farm and riding through the hills with me. At breakfast and supper we would talk about me spending the winter at the Cheyenne village, while Ma and Pa tried to ignore the hints we threw around so freely. After two and a half days of hints and suggestions, my parents finally consented. It didn't take long to put together the few things I would need. "I'll be careful," I said for the tenth time that morning, "we'll be back in the spring, and Runs with the Wind is going to stay here with us for a while."

Ma watched as we rode off through the valley, toward the Cheyenne's winter camp.

"He sure has grown up," she said trying to hide her doubts and fears.

You see, Ma wasn't to happy about the idea at first, but at least now I had that high snow covered peak above the cabin to always show me the way home.

SNEAK PREVIEW OF BOOK TWO
SPIRIT OF THE BUFFALO

Chapter One

"I will be careful ma, trust me," Jeremy found himself saying for the tenth time that morning. They had gone over it so many times that he was becoming more than a little irritated at his mother's constant worrying. Since the very moment that his parents had agreed to let him go spend the winter with his adopted Cheyenne family, she had become more and more apprehensive, coming up with one excuse after another why he shouldn't go. Only the argument of spending time with his relatives had finally convinced her, and that had been a flimsy argument at best.

He and his blood brother, Runs with the Wind, had done everything possible to calm her fears by describing how quiet and peaceful a snowed in Cheyenne winter camp was. Though he knew very little about it himself, Runs with the Wind had coached him well on precisely what points to bring up. He assured her that the two of them would be spending long days and nights in the lodge of his adopted father, Night Hawk, learning the ways of the spirits and the medicine man. Surely there would be no trouble for them to get into, even if they tried.

Cheryl raised her hand and opened her mouth to call out to her son one more time, as the two boys rode away from the cabin through the slowly falling snow. The valley floor was almost totally white, surrounded on all sides by the dark green of the pine trees. All the crops had been harvested, and enough wild grass had been cut and put up to get the horses through the winter. There were several cords of wood stacked in the lean-to, and there was plenty of dried and canned meat in the root cellar to get them through the winter, so even she couldn't put her finger on what it was that made her so unwilling to let him leave.

"Let him go dear," John said, placing a reassuring hand on his wife's shoulder. "He's in good hands, besides the snow will be to deep for them to get into any mischief before you know it."

Just then the two boys let out a wild war whoop and raced headlong down the valley to be swallowed up by the early winter storm.

A sudden shiver went down Cheryl's spine as a forbidding feeling overwhelmed her. Had she been able to reach her son at that moment, she would have snatched him out of the saddle and dragged him, kicking and screaming if necessary, back to the safety of the cabin. This was going to be a long winter, and even the warm smile on her husband's face couldn't wash away the apprehension she felt as she tried to get one last glimpse of her departing son.

Jeremy, on the other hand, felt nothing but sheer exhilaration as the wind whipped at his face and the tiny snowflakes stuck to his eyelashes making it hard to see. Every moment he spent with the Cheyenne people seemed to awaken the senses of his spirit, and stir up deeply buried emotions from beyond the reaches of his memory. Each story of the old days, which Night Hawk told so masterfully, could create such images in his head, that he felt he was actually a part of it. "Yes," Jeremy thought, "this is going to be anything but boring."

As they reached the end of the valley Runs with the Wind swung his horse off of the trail and headed south along a well used game trail.

"Hey, brother, I thought you said your camp was more to the east?"

"It is."

"Then why are we going south?"

"Because that's where the buffalo are, and you

wouldn't want to miss the last big hunt of the season would you?"

"Why didn't you mention it before?"

"Do you think your mother and father would have let you come if they had known?"

"Probably not," Jeremy replied.

"This way your mother won't have something else to worry about."

"I guess you're right," Jeremy said, squirming slightly in his saddle as though he could feel his mother watching him.

"Well, are we going to sit here in the snow all day, or are we going to hunt buffalo?"

"We're going hunting of course, but are you sure we can catch the main hunting party?"

"We're going to get there first," Runs with the Wind said, beginning to lay out his plan. "The big herd is two days ride south of the village and the hunters will be moving slow so they don't spook the stragglers. We'll ride fast, staying to the west so we can get ahead of the buffalo and cut off their escape. We'll find a safe spot to set up an ambush where the buffalo will come right past us. With my bow and your rifle, and the buffalo so close, we should take many animals for our fathers lodge. Our people will be singing our praises all through the season of snow."

"What if we accidentally spook the buffalo first?"

"Then they run back toward the winter camp, and the main hunting party takes them by surprise closer to home. Either way, we can't lose."

"Seems like you got this all figured out," Jeremy said, sounding more convinced than he really was, "so what are we waiting for?"

On they rode, not realizing this was going to be the biggest test of their survival skills, and the toughest winter either one of them had ever faced.

BOOK ORDER FORM

Please send me the following books:

	Qty.	Price	Total
Runs with the Wind	_____	$6.95	_____
Spirit of the Buffalo	_____	$6.95	_____
Coming soon Zeb's Revenge			

For products shipped to Arizona please
add 7.4%=$0.51 cents sales tax   _____

Shipping and Handling
$2.50 for first book and $1.00 for
each additional book
For orders of 10 or more please contact publisher

BOOK ORDER TOTAL   _____

Please ship books to (your address):

Name _____

Address _____

City, State, Zip _____

Please mail order form and check or money order to:

Renegade Publishing
P.O. Box 544
Camp Verde, AZ 86322
books@RenegadePublishing.com

BOOK ORDER FORM

Please send me the following books:

	Qty.	Price	Total
Runs with the Wind	_____	$6.95	_____
Spirit of the Buffalo	_____	$6.95	_____
Coming soon Zeb's Revenge			

For products shipped to Arizona please
add 7.4%=$0.51 cents sales tax   _____

Shipping and Handling
$2.50 for first book and $1.00 for
each additional book
<u>For orders of 10 or more please contact publisher</u>

BOOK ORDER TOTAL   _____

Please ship books to (your address):

Name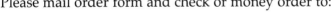

Address _____

City, State, Zip _____

Please mail order form and check or money order to:

Renegade Publishing
P.O. Box 544
Camp Verde, AZ 86322
books@RenegadePublishing.com

BOOK ORDER FORM

Please send me the following books:

	Qty.	Price	Total
Runs with the Wind	_____	$6.95	_____
Spirit of the Buffalo	_____	$6.95	_____
Coming soon Zeb's Revenge			

For products shipped to Arizona please
add 7.4%=$0.51 cents sales tax   _____

Shipping and Handling
$2.50 for first book and $1.00 for
each additional book
<u>For orders of 10 or more please contact publisher</u>

BOOK ORDER TOTAL   _____

Please ship books to (your address):

Name   _____

Address   _____

City, State, Zip   _____

Please mail order form and check or money order to:

Renegade Publishing
P.O. Box 544
Camp Verde, AZ 86322
books@RenegadePublishing.com

BOOK ORDER FORM

Please send me the following books:

	Qty.	Price	Total
Runs with the Wind	_____	$6.95	_____
Spirit of the Buffalo	_____	$6.95	_____
Coming soon Zeb's Revenge			

For products shipped to Arizona please
add 7.4%=$0.51 cents sales tax   _____

Shipping and Handling
$2.50 for first book and $1.00 for
each additional book
For orders of 10 or more please contact publisher

BOOK ORDER TOTAL   _____

Please ship books to (your address):

Name   _____

Address   _____

City, State, Zip   _____

Please mail order form and check or money order to:

Renegade Publishing
P.O. Box 544
Camp Verde, AZ 86322
books@RenegadePublishing.com